PURRAMID SCHEME

A WHISKERS AND WORDS MYSTERY
BOOK SEVEN

ERYN SCOTT

KRISTOPHERSON
PRESS
Publishing

This victim left the town of Button in *tiers*.

Button residents are normally as wary of pyramid schemes as the next town. But when Vicki Younger comes to town, promising a miracle serum, locals jump at the chance to invest in her business. When everyone loses their money, and Vicki shows up dead, the town is in hot water—especially one of Lou's regulars, Silas, who was seen angrily following Vicki mere minutes before she died.

While Silas doesn't deny his anger, or how he'd been shadowing Vicki, he swears he wasn't the one to end her life. Sure her friend is telling the truth, Lou asks him to recount Vicki's activities during her last hours. What Silas describes is odd, to say the least, even inexplicable at times, which definitely doesn't help his plea of innocence. Can Lou untangle the clues and lead them to the true killer before Silas is put away for the rest of his days?

Welcome to Button

1 - Whiskers and Words
2 - Willow's Nursery
3 - Button Bistro
4 - Scoop O' Button
5 - George's Technology Emporium
6 - Bean and Button Coffeehouse
7 - Willow and Easton's houses
8 - Material Girls
9 - The Upholstered Button
10 - Old Mansion
11 - Bank
12 - Pet Store
13 - Bakery

CHAPTER I

L ouisa Henry exhaled a contented breath as a cool breeze blew through the muggy bookshop. Each of the customers inside stopped and closed their eyes for a moment, letting the relief flow over them. It was mid-June, and temperatures were already creeping up, turning Lou's beloved bookshop into a veritable oven on hot days.

"That screen door makes such a difference," George said. As a regular, the young woman knew the store almost as well as Lou.

"I know." Lou chuckled. "I've never felt so excited about a door before in my life."

"Did you install it by yourself?" George asked, regarding the door.

Lou shook her head. "Noah drove by after closing the clinic last night and saw me struggling with it."

Noah, the local veterinarian didn't usually pass by her bookshop on his way home, so she was grateful for the serendipitous situation as well as his help.

"He's coming back tonight to install another one at the

back door so we can get a cross-breeze going. There wasn't time for us to install both yesterday." Lou checked her watch. It was only a half hour before she was set to close, and Noah was supposed to show up around dinnertime.

Silas, another bookshop regular, flipped a gold dollar coin between his fingers as he read his newspaper. "It's a good thing you're getting it done tonight. Starting tomorrow, Noah's going to be busier than a moth in a wool sweater store with all that quilting nonsense."

Lou would have to take Silas's word for it. Last year, Lou's first summer in Button, Noah's family hadn't held their annual quilting convention. But if the buzz and commotion leading up to this year's event were any indication of the busyness, the whole town was about to be overtaken by quilting enthusiasts.

Silas was right. That made Noah's help with the screen doors even more selfless. He didn't have the time, but he still made her a priority. Well, her and the cats.

After all, the cats were the reason she'd needed the screen door in the first place. Unlike some of the other businesses in the downtown section of Button, Lou couldn't just prop her front door open when the thermometer started edging into the eighties. As good as the bookshop cats were about steering clear of the door, they couldn't be trusted not to venture outside if it was propped open, especially not her newest foster, Catticus Finch.

As if he knew she was thinking about him, the troublemaker took that opportunity to vault off the top of one of the tall bookshelves and land on another. The bookshop customers held their collective breath as they waited for him to regain his balance and strut away from the jump as if it were nothing.

"That cat's gonna give me a heart attack," George said, placing a hand over her heart.

"Tell me about it," Lou mumbled. "He overshot one of the bookshelves yesterday and fell. He managed to flip his body around at the very last second, but I was convinced he was going to be the first cat who didn't land on his feet."

Forrest, her final regular, clicked his tongue and patted Anne Mice's head where they both sat on the love seat in the middle of the shop. "Your twin is out of control," he told the cat in his baritone voice.

The two cats were twins in appearance only. They were both striking gray tabbies, but where Anne Mice was laid back and sweet, Catticus was wild and playful. A cat in need was a cat in need, though, and when the owner of the ice cream shop next door had found Catticus scrounging around in her dumpster one afternoon, Lou had gladly added him to her happy feline herd.

Silas sniffed distastefully. "The breeze from that screen door is nice, but now I think it's letting in too much of the smell from those jasmine plants." He dropped the coin he'd been fiddling with back into his pocket and pulled out the monogrammed handkerchief he kept on him at all times. A great trumpeting noise filled the bookstore as he blew his nose, scaring a few of the cats.

"I think it's nice," Lou said in defense of the jasmine plants her best friend had loaned her from her nursery up the street.

"I might've agreed with you until a few weeks ago, but

lately jasmine just reminds me of bad decisions," Silas grumbled.

"Come on, Silas." Lou tipped her head to one side. "You can't keep beating yourself up for that."

Silas had been one of many townspeople who'd recently fallen prey to a pyramid investment scheme centered around a facial serum that smelled like jasmine and had promised smoother, younger-looking skin in just a few weeks. And even though it had seemed too good to be true, it was the company's owner who turned out to be the fake instead of the serum.

Vicki Younger had blown into town about two months prior looking for investors in exchange for shares of what she promised would become a multi-million-dollar company.

There were no signs Vicki would run. She'd been in the process of buying a house in the town next door. And even though she'd complained that she fit in better in Button and wished she'd shopped around a little more before committing to a house in Brine, the locals assured her they wouldn't hold it against her.

"Lou's the only smart one here," Silas said, folding down his newspaper and sticking it on the couch next to him. "She said no from the beginning."

While Silas was the only one of Lou's regulars who'd gone through with the investment, Forrest and George had both strongly considered it, finding the promise of owning shares of the business tempting. In the end, they had both decided not to invest, but it had been close.

"Vicki fooled a lot of people, not just you." Forrest's tone was calming, as was always the case with the local psychologist. But Lou had a terrible feeling it wouldn't be able to calm everyone in Vicki Younger's wake.

"Yeah," Lou chimed in. "I only shied away from the opportunity because Ben was the one who handled our investments."

At first, Lou had wondered if her inability to think about investments was a setback in the moving-on process after losing her husband suddenly to a heart attack. But her hesitation turned out to be the thing that stopped Lou from losing some of her savings to Vicki's scam.

"It was such an excellent product," Lou added. "You couldn't have known."

Vicki's product, Snail Serum X, really *had been* amazing. Despite being immediately wary at the thought of putting something that came from a snail on her face, Lou had given in and tried a sample. Vicki had gone into detail about the humane process the company used to collect the mucin by having a snail spa where they sat in a pleasant steam bath while the lab collected the wrinkle-fighting mucin.

"On that positive note..." George stood and said, "I should head home soon. I have a date to get ready for tonight."

Lou blinked. Silas coughed in surprise. Even the unflappable Forrest moved the cat off his lap as if he might stand up.

"What? With whom?" Lou sputtered out the questions.

As long as she'd known George, the young woman had never talked about dating anyone. She seemed perfectly content to act as the tech support for the town, play her online video games, walk around with her beloved cat strapped to her like a baby, and take part in her weekly Dungeons and Dragons group.

Lifting her chin as if she might avoid the questions, George turned like she was about to leave. "He's just some guy I met online."

At that comment, Silas was the one who got to his feet instead of Forrest. "Online?" Silas spat out the word as if it were poisonous. "How can you possibly think that's safe? If the last few weeks have taught me anything, it's that you can't trust anyone." Silas crossed his arms and harrumphed.

Forrest held up a hand to calm the fuming older man. "George is a smart, capable person. We can trust her to make her own decisions."

George bowed her head toward Forrest to show him she was grateful for his support. "Me dating a guy I met online isn't the same as what Vicki pulled," George spoke up, getting everyone back on topic. "Plus, he's from Brine, so he doesn't even live that far away."

"Are you sure he *actually* lives in Brine?" Silas asked, referencing the fact that they'd found out—too late—that Vicki had been lying about buying a house there. He snapped his fingers. "It's too bad Brine doesn't have their own *BSB* so we could check out this guy George is dating. You know? Make sure he's never been mentioned."

The *BSB*, or *Behind the Scenes Button*, was a blog that shared all the gossip about the town of Button and the people who lived there. The blogger's identity was anonymous, and they operated under the tagline, *Everything you won't read in the* Button Post. The blog had started just a few months ago, advertised on a series of flyers that showed up on local bulletin boards.

"The *BSB* doesn't know everything," Forrest reminded Silas.

Lou motioned to Forrest to emphasize his point. "Yes, I stand by my feeling that the *BSB* shouldn't be trusted. Whoever they are, they obviously don't have the town's best interest at heart."

The *BSB* had lost her support when their first post had been all about the supposed *real* reason behind the cancellation of last year's annual quilting convention. The story the town was told was that the park, where the convention had always been held, had been going through some much-needed drainage work to prevent the field from flooding each fall. But the *BSB* hypothesized that Rosa Ramero, the owner of the local quilt shop, had actually been on the verge of bankruptcy.

Even though Lou didn't know Rosa that well, her son Noah was one of Lou's closest acquaintances in town. Lou hadn't heard anything about Noah's family quilt shop being in trouble, and while she knew that was private information that Noah might not necessarily divulge, Material Girls seemed to be even busier than ever.

"Right. The *BSB* never said anything about Vicki directly. There was just that one post about the Snail Serum X investment opportunity," George reminded Silas. Apparently, she'd gotten sucked in by the conversation because she seemed to have forgotten all about leaving.

Silas harrumphed. "I suppose you're right. I just don't know how the *BSB* let that kind of gossip get past them."

"Maybe because the *BSB* was Vicki, and they've stopped

posting because she's gone." Forrest lifted one thick eyebrow in a show of skepticism.

"See? That's what I think." As if to pull up evidence to back up her point, George grabbed her phone and poked at the screen. Her eyes widened. "Okay, well, I take that back. There's a new post. The *BSB* has not only broken their streak against talking about Vicki, but they also say she's back in town."

"What?" Silas stopped his pacing and turned to look at George.

The younger woman checked her phone again, as if she might've misread it the first time. "*BSB* says Vicki was spotted by the bank about fifteen minutes ago. She slunk around the corner, and they lost sight of her, but she's around."

"So she's back?" Forrest asked, his expression brightening. "That could mean she didn't run away with your money after all."

Silas huffed. "Just like the psychologist to think the best of everyone. If she's not hiding anything, why is she sneaking around?"

Forrest squinted one eye and nodded an admission of defeat.

Placing his hands on his hips, Silas harrumphed. "That's it. Enough standing around. I'm going to confront the weasel and make her pay me back."

"How are you going to do that?" George asked.

Silas pressed his lips into a grim line. "I'm not sure at the moment, but mark my words, I'll get my revenge on that little sneak. And I'll get my money back, no matter what it takes." With that, he stormed out of the bookshop.

CHAPTER 2

Lou had planned on waiting until later to go on a run, preferring the cooler temperatures once the sun started to set. But after learning of Vicki's return to town, and seeing her regulars all scatter shortly after, Lou found she needed a run to clear her head right after closing the shop that evening.

Slipping into shorts and a tank top, Lou warmed up by jogging once around the exterior of the bookshop. She planned her route as she stretched next to the jasmine plants. Lou knew many runners who preferred to run a set route each time they worked out. Ben had been one of those runners, loving his normal pathway through Central Park because it helped him to keep track of his pacing. But Lou had always preferred to change things up. And even though Button was a small town, not allowing for too many variations on running routes, she tried her best to see different things each time she ran.

Maybe I'll try running in the woods today, Lou thought as she stretched down to loosen her hamstring. *The fact that the closest trail is in the woods behind the bank, where Vicki was last sighted, is merely a coincidence, right?*

Lou headed down Thimble Drive and then took a left on Linen Street. She normally avoided the place since James, the manager, was Willow's ex-fiancé and one of Lou's least favorite people ever since she'd found out he'd been cheating on Willow.

Running into James or Vicki seemed out of the question, though, because as Lou jogged past the bank, there wasn't a single car in the parking lot.

If Vicki was here, Silas probably scared her off, Lou told herself with a shiver, remembering how he'd left the bookshop in a huff about a half hour earlier. *I wouldn't stick around either if I were her.*

Vicki or no, Lou still liked the idea of jogging through the woods since her skin already shone with sweat. She jogged through the bank parking lot and took the path that led into the wooded area that took up the rest of the block, loving the change of soft earth under her feet instead of the hard pavement. But Lou's happiness waned as she rounded a bend in the trail and found a small clearing in the forest. A red hatchback was parked in the space, even though there didn't seem to be a road leading to the area.

Lou recognized that car. Each time Vicki had driven into town to hang out with them, she'd climbed out of a very similar red hatchback. Hesitant but curious, Lou ran closer to make sure. There didn't appear to be anyone in the car at first glance, so Lou peered into the window.

She screamed. Lying face up in the backseat of the sedan with her eyes wide open and unblinking was Vicki Younger.

LOU RAN her hands up and down her arms as she paced in the woods near the car after calling the police. It was still hot, but finding Vicki dead gave Lou a chill even the warm sun and exercise couldn't touch. She kept the body behind her, not wanting to stray too far while she waited for help to arrive, but also not particularly wanting to see the lifeless look in the woman's eyes any more than she had to.

Guilt swarmed her thoughts like angry bees. She hadn't been able to bring herself to open the car door, let alone touch the woman to check for signs of life. She didn't doubt the woman was dead, though. The way she hadn't reacted at all to Lou's scream and the marks around her neck told that story loud and clear.

It wasn't until Detective Anderson's dark sedan bumped to a stop along the forest path that Lou remembered Easton was out of town. He and Willow were off on their first week-long getaway together, so of course Roy would be the one to answer the call instead of Easton.

Seeing Detective Roy Anderson climb out of the driver's side of his unmarked sedan, followed by another cruiser of crime scene technicians, didn't fill Lou with dread like it usually did. Ever since he and a local high school teacher Carly Zimmerman had begun dating, he was much less snarky and a lot less likely to see the bad in everyone involved in a situation.

"Is that who I think it is?" Roy asked, his gaze flicking over to the car as he stopped to talk to Lou while the crime scene team went over to check out the body.

Lou swallowed the unpleasant taste that cropped up in

her mouth at the thought of the dead woman sitting behind her. "Vicki."

Roy's throat bobbed as his dark eyebrows lowered. "Please tell me she's not strangled."

"How'd you know?" Lou glanced over her shoulder, confirming the fact that Vicki's body wasn't visible from that distance.

"Because I got no less than five calls over the past hour telling me that people had seen Silas following her and threatening to 'wring her neck.'" Roy's nostrils flared with frustration.

Lou cringed as she remembered the threats Silas made before he rushed out of the bookshop. "So people actually saw him following her around? Did he confront her?"

"I guess I'll find out when I question him." But instead of making it sound like he was sure Silas was guilty, Roy's flat tone spoke more of the frustration he felt that he even *had* to consider the old man a suspect.

It was a pleasant change in the detective. The last few cases she'd been involved with, he'd jumped to the easiest conclusion, badgering the people who were the first on the scene as if they'd orchestrated the whole thing to avoid suspicion.

"Can you tell me how you came upon her?" Roy asked, turning toward the car and waving for her to follow.

Lou only hesitated for a moment before trailing him over to the crime scene. "I was on a run." Pausing, she realized she would need to come clean about the reason she was in the area. "I'll admit I took a route that went past the bank after hearing there had been a Vicki sighting there." She cleared her throat as they approached the car. "I thought it might be nice to run in the woods since it was hot, and the trees might give me a little shade. Her car wasn't hard to spot once I'd run a ways down the path."

Roy jotted down a few notes on a pad he pulled from his pocket. "So that was around five thirty?" he asked.

"Yes," Lou confirmed, glancing down at the ground. There, next to her sneakers, was the same gold dollar coin she'd seen Silas flipping less than an hour ago in her shop. "Oh no," Lou groaned.

Roy leaned down and surveyed the coin. "Officer Little, can you bring me an evidence bag, please?" he barked out at a nearby officer. "Based on your reaction, I'm guessing this is going to have Silas Owings's fingerprints all over it?"

Lou chewed on her bottom lip.

Officer Little came over, holding out the requested bag and noting the coin on the ground. "Did you say Silas Owings?" When Roy nodded, the officer said, "We found a handkerchief in the car with the initials S.O. on it. It was stuck in the back driver's side door like it got caught."

Lou and Roy shared a worried glance. Lou wasn't sure if Roy knew the significance, but Silas carried one of those every day. This was looking more and more problematic for her regular.

"Thank you, Officer Little." Roy took the evidence bag and waved the man away. He donned a glove before bending to pick up the coin. Once it was safely in the bag, Roy shook his head. "Easton sure picked the wrong week to go out of town."

"Or the right one," Lou scoffed.

Roy let out a dry laugh. "Where'd they go again?"

"A little town in the Cascade Valley called Stoneybrook?" Lou phrased it as a question mostly because she'd never heard of the place, which wasn't strictly a surprise since she'd lived on the East Coast for the last two decades. "Willow said it's supercute, and there's a ton of shopping, hiking, and whitewater rafting."

Willow had needed the list of all the amenities before agreeing to go, reluctant to leave her nursery for the week. But after three months of being at Valley Nursery sunup to sundown while the business got on its feet, Easton, Lou, and Peggy Lee—Willow's business partner—all agreed that the woman needed a break. And while Willow had been excited about the prospect of shopping and visiting the town's year-long farmers market, the option to lodge her horse and pygmy goat in the barn at the local bed-and-breakfast had officially sold her on the vacation. Being able to take her horse and his goat best friend with her for the trip had been the deciding factor. It didn't hurt that there would be a horse for Easton to rent so he could take trail rides through the valley alongside Willow and OC.

While she thought about it all, Lou's body relaxed from the tense state it had been in since she'd found Vicki. Lou glanced at Roy, who was watching her. He'd remembered the place just fine. He'd asked to get Lou's mind off the trauma of finding a dead body.

As if he knew he'd been caught, Roy swiped at the sweat forming on his forehead in the heat. "I know I'm not Easton, but I'm going to do everything I can to clear Silas."

Lou swallowed her fears and doubts. "Thank you, Roy."

"I'll let you know if I have any more questions." He focused on the car, his jaw tightening as he looked at the body once more.

Lou couldn't quite make herself turn around to leave.

"Hey..." Roy caught her gaze. "With the public nature of his threats, and his possessions littered all over my crime scene, I've got to look into him."

"I understand." Lou sighed.

"Given how many people around here were mad at her, it shouldn't be too hard to find someone else who wanted her dead," Roy added.

She hoped he was right. Regardless, she couldn't help the bad feeling that buried itself in her gut, making her feel queasy as she walked away.

It wasn't just Silas, though he was at the forefront of her worries. The quilt convention was set to start tomorrow, and families were supposed to be celebrating the end of school for the summer. News of Vicki's murder was about to settle over Button like a muggy, inescapable heat wave.

Lou had a bad feeling that no amount of screen doors or cross-breezes would help this scandal blow through town any faster.

CHAPTER 3

Ever since Lou had moved to Button, Whiskers and Words had been a sanctuary for her. It was the first place she felt at home after losing Ben. She'd grown to see the bookshop and her apartment above as a place to catch her when she fell.

That feeling only intensified as she returned home from her run-turned-wrong.

The bookshop seemed to whisper its support, the cats winked at her in greeting from their respective napping spots throughout the warm space, and the smell of the books—new and old—felt like a comfortable quilt wrapped around her shoulders.

Sweaty from the run back home, Lou kept the door open and latched the screen door so the breeze would make its way through the building that had gotten a little stuffy in her absence. She closed her eyes, lifting her arms slightly so the cool breeze might air out her armpits.

A man cleared his throat.

Lou's eyes snapped open, heat automatically rushing to

her cheeks when she saw it was Noah standing on the other side of the screen door. His tool belt hugged his hips, strapped over khaki shorts and a moss-green T-shirt that brought out the hazel notes in his brown eyes. His dimples deepened as he smirked at the state he'd found her in.

"Omigosh, Noah. I forgot you were coming over to install the other door." She suctioned her arms back to her sides and rushed forward to open the screen door for him.

He chuckled. "I got that feeling," he said, stepping into the bookshop as she held open the door.

Placing a hand on her sweaty forehead, she tried to explain. "I went for a run, and I would've had plenty of time to make it back here before you arrived, but..." Lou swallowed, not sure she knew how to continue that sentence.

Noah's dark eyebrows pulled together as he sensed her unease. "Is everything okay?"

Lou shook her head. "I found Vicki." The woman's name was broken as it escaped her lips, leaving no room for interpretation. "She was..."

"Dead?" Noah asked, showing the emotion backing Lou's words had done its job to convey the dire situation.

"Strangled," Lou croaked out the word even though her throat felt like it had a hand wrapped around it just like someone had done to Vicki.

Before Lou could figure out what was happening, Noah stepped forward, wrapping her up in a tight hug. "Are you okay?" he asked. Quickly, he added, "Of course you aren't. I'm so sorry. Can I get you anything? Do you want some water?"

Even though she was a sweaty mess from her run, Lou's

self-conscious thoughts melted away in Noah's embrace. She felt like a nervous cat, settling into a relaxed puddle once it was being cradled in his strong arms.

"Water sounds good," she croaked into his arm as he hugged her tight.

Stepping back, but not without keeping a steadying hand on each of her shoulders until he was sure she could stand upright on her own, Noah looked toward the back office where he knew a small kitchen held essential items she used throughout the day.

"I'll be right back," he said, rushing over to the office and returning a moment later with a cup of cool water from the tap.

Lou gulped it down and settled in one of the chairs around the table in the front window, suddenly realizing her knees were a little weak. Noah sat next to her.

"You don't have to talk about it." Noah leaned forward, monitoring the level in her glass of water, as if he were ready to hop up and get her more the second she needed it.

"It's okay." It was getting easier to breathe. "I shouldn't have taken the path in the woods behind the bank," she added when Noah frowned in question.

"You saw the *BSB* post?" Noah guessed.

"The regulars were talking about it right before I closed the shop for the day, and I … I couldn't help myself, I guess. Finding a body is exactly what I deserve for being nosy." She shook her head, disappointed in herself for giving in to such a curious impulse.

Noah's hand covered hers. He squeezed tight. "Don't beat yourself up. It's human nature. Plus, it's good you found her. Out there in the woods, she could've gone days before she was found. This way, Roy can get started figuring out who did this. Did he have any leads?"

Lou flinched. "Silas is the only one I know about."

"Silas?" The tightness in Noah's jaw mirrored the discomfort Lou felt.

"He made a ton of threats about making her pay back the money she stole and was seen following her this afternoon." Lou wished she couldn't see the grumpy old man wrapping his hands around her neck in a fit of anger. But the truth was, as sweet as Silas *could* be, he was also ornery and easily angered. And the threat she'd witnessed had seemed like something he'd make good on if given the chance.

"I still can't believe Silas invested in the first place." Noah blinked in surprise.

Lou nodded. She, too, had been surprised that the seventy-something man would be interested in investing in a skincare product. "He said his granddaughters are really getting into anti-wrinkle products now that they're in their thirties." Lou snorted. As someone who was closing in on forty, she could only laugh when younger people acted like being in their thirties felt like they were closing in on their deathbed.

"He thought it would bring them closer." Noah seemed to understand the inclination. His daughter was in her preteen years, and he was constantly trying to keep up with her changing likes and dislikes.

Lou finished her water but held up her hand when Noah stood to get her more. "I'm okay. Thanks. Should we get to work on the back door? I can't wait to see what it feels like in here with the cross-breeze. The front one feels so good already."

"I saw." Noah smirked.

This time, the heat that flushed over Lou was less from embarrassment and more from the way Noah's eyes traveled over her.

She realized, at that moment, she was still wearing her short running shorts and a tank top. But any impulse to change into something with more coverage was quashed by the memory of the first screen door they'd put up together. It had been hard, sweaty work, and Lou didn't want to change if she was just going to get gross all over again.

"I propped the other screen door in the back hallway." Lou stood, needing a distraction from Noah's intense gaze. "Should I get started on the measurements?"

"Sounds good." Noah handed over his tape measure from his tool belt. "I'm sure this one will go in much more quickly." He winked.

Calling Noah for help with the front door hadn't been Lou's first impulse upon getting the screen doors delivered, unfortunately. Even though it had turned out to be a positive thing in the end, the reminder that she'd shied away from the investment opportunity because it was *Ben's thing* had hit her harder than she thought it would. She'd moped around for a few evenings as she thought about how moving on from his death needed to include her not relying on a partner to take on half of the jobs in life anymore. She needed to do everything for herself.

Which, apparently, included purchasing and hanging screen doors for the bookshop.

The ordering had been easy enough. And the hardware

store delivered them to her doorstep for a small fee, which was great since Willow was out of town with her truck. But after three straight hours and multiple attempts to get the door to hang and close correctly, she'd finally asked for help.

Well, more accurately, Noah had been walking by and had offered her a helping hand last night on his way home from the clinic. And while she may have been too proud to ask for help in the first place, she wasn't against accepting it when it was offered.

Her gaze dropped at the reminder of the predicament her pride had gotten her into. "Yes, and this one will require fewer holes drilled in the wrong places," she admitted.

"Don't beat yourself up too bad," Noah said. "You should've seen the first few times I used a power drill." He let out one of his signature deep laughs. "It was a disaster."

"Well, thank you, really. I truly appreciate your help. And I know you won't let me pay you." She waited as he nodded in confirmation that it was still the case. "But please know I'm always here for you if you need anything."

Noah's eyes lit up at her statement. "Actually, there is something you could do for me."

Surprised that he was asking for a favor, Lou blinked. "Sure. Anything."

"My Aunt Cricket is back in town, as of this week, after being on the East Coast for a couple of years," he explained.

Noah had two aunts who lived locally, Bianca and Elena, and he referred to each of them as *Tia*, never *Aunt*.

His cheeks turned red as he must've caught Lou's confusion. "She's not *technically* related to me, just a very close friend of the family."

Lou smiled in understanding.

"Anyway, she's dying to meet you, and I'd love for you to check out the convention tomorrow. Would you meet me there?" Noah studied her, waiting for her answer.

"Of course," she said, honored that he wanted her to meet such an important person in his life.

"Great." He beamed. "Does after you close the shop tomorrow work? I'll be there most of the day. I had Kathleen block out this week for me in advance this year, so I don't have any appointments at the clinic. I can be on hand for whatever they need."

"Sounds great," Lou answered.

With that taken care of, they went to work hanging the second screen door. Lou moved the cats upstairs so they wouldn't have to worry about them getting in the way of the installation or slipping through the open doorway while they worked. After that, they worked together to install the screen, making sure it closed correctly and locked from the inside since she didn't want customers entering through the back alley. As they worked, Noah chatted about Cricket and how she'd been his mother's best friend since before he was born.

"The two of them kind of remind me of you and Willow," he said, checking the door to make sure it swung in and out without hindrance.

"And she's been gone for a few years?" Lou asked, putting away the tools they'd used.

He dipped his head. "Yeah, her husband got a job opportunity on the East Coast that he couldn't pass up, so they moved there while he completed the contract. But they're back now, hopefully for good. I know Mom really missed her."

Lou knew all about the lovely feeling of living nearby a best friend after years away. She gathered the plastic wrapping that had covered the door and hugged it to her, flattening it further so she could toss it in the back dumpster.

"Thank you." She closed her eyes as the cross-breeze she'd been dreaming about automatically kicked in, swirling through the shop and around her.

"Anytime." Noah's tone was so light and dreamy Lou had to open her eyes to see what he was looking at.

But his eyes were closed, too, and he was standing in the cool air just like she had been. Beads of sweat clung to his temples, just like the ones Lou had been swiping away throughout the last hour. Lou's face felt hot as she gulped. Taking advantage of his eyes being closed, she took the chance to stare at him a little, something she didn't get the opportunity to do very often.

She'd always known Noah was handsome. His brown skin, dimples, dark features, and bright smile were classically good looking. Added to his burly physique, he was quite possibly the "total package" so many women talked about: strong *and* sensitive. But it was his personality that had made the biggest difference. It was his quiet confidence, the calming presence he exuded, that really made him attractive to her.

So attractive, in fact, that she'd been feeling a little tongue-tied and giddy around him lately.

Noah cracked an eye open, catching her staring. He smirked. Flustered, Lou hugged the bundle of plastic wrapping tighter, causing the air trapped inside to poof up into her face. She felt like a teenager with a school-yard crush all over again, unsure how to act and worried she was misreading every sign. It had been a long time since she'd dated. She and Ben had gotten together in college and had been together ever since. Lou had hoped it would instinctively come back to her, but the self-doubt crept in, making her apprehensive.

Among the millions of hesitations swirling through her mind, one of the bigger ones was that Lou didn't want to ruin a great friendship she'd grown to depend on over the past year and a half.

"We should let the cats out," Lou said in a desperate attempt to change the subject. She lunged for the door that closed off the stairs from the bookshop. Cats streamed through the open doorway, proving they'd all been waiting there while she and Noah worked. Lou rocked back on her heels. "Well, thank you so much for your help. I won't keep you any longer if you have something to do."

Noah's lips parted as if he were about to say something, but Lou's phone rang, interrupting him.

"Sorry," she said as she fished the thing from the pocket of her running shorts. She frowned at the screen. "It says it's the Button Police Department."

"Maybe Roy has more questions for you." Noah shrugged.

That had to be it. Lou answered, "Hello?"

"Lou? It's Silas. I need you to come bail me out of jail. I've been arrested."

CHAPTER 4

L ou and Noah rushed into the police station minutes later. Lou had been ready to grab her purse and run down there, but Noah had convinced her to let him drive.

The first sensation she experienced upon stepping foot in the station was the cool air. Air-conditioning. Even though her new screen doors had created some much-needed relief from the heat, the blast of air-conditioned air was a whole different level of comfort.

The second sensation Lou felt was disappointment. Reynolds, the ornery officer who manned the front desk, sat waiting for them in the lobby. He took one look at her running outfit and sneered as if she should've been wearing something more suitable just in case her friend got arrested and needed to be bailed out of jail.

The sneer Reynolds wore faded as he caught sight of Noah behind Lou. From her experience with the rest of the town, Reynolds might've been scared of Noah—the man was rather intimidating in size and stature—or he could simply respect the man. Being the town vet meant he'd helped a lot of the locals' beloved pets, earning him an air of deference around Button that Lou had most recently discovered between him and Detective Anderson. Even though Roy would barely give Lou the time of day when they'd first met at a crime scene, the sour detective had straightened up and shown Noah more respect than Lou had previously thought him capable of.

"Dr. Ramero," Officer Reynolds said after inclining his head toward them. "What can I help you with?"

Noah shot an incredulous look at the officer, then looked at Lou. He gestured toward her, letting Reynolds know he would have to talk to her instead of him.

"Silas Owings is being held here. Can we talk to him?" Lou stepped forward, pushing past her frustration with Reynolds in favor of helping Silas. He needed to be her priority.

"Oh, the strangler?" Officer Reynolds asked as casually as if he were talking about something other than cold-blooded murder. Then he added, "Yeah, he's with Detective Anderson."

Lou blinked at his crassness. "Can you let the detective know we're here?" She pushed the question out through gritted teeth, knowing it wouldn't help to yell at the snarky officer as much as she wanted to.

No, she needed to save that anger for Detective Anderson. What had happened? Had he lied to her about trying to investigate other suspects? Was it all a ruse to placate her so she would leave his crime scene earlier?

While Lou fumed, Officer Reynolds rolled his eyes and picked up the phone, mumbling something into the receiver about visitors before placing the phone back into the cradle. "You can head on back. I'm sure you know the way by now." He flicked a disinterested hand toward the detectives' offices.

Lou shot him a quick glare before hoofing it down the hall. She heard Noah thank him before following behind. Detective Anderson had obviously been the one whom Reynolds had called a moment before because he was already standing behind his desk in preparation for company.

"What's going on?" The question burst out of Lou as she entered the office. "You arrested him?"

Roy frowned. "What? No. I just brought him in for questioning. He's free to leave after this. I asked him to call you here because I need your help with something."

"Oh." Lou's frustration transferred from Roy to Silas even though he wasn't in the room. Then she reminded herself that the older man had gone through a lot that day, and she should cut him some slack too. "What can I help with?"

Lou sank into one of the two chairs situated across from the detective. Noah settled into the other. Roy followed suit, though he perched on the edge of his chair as if he still might need to be on the defensive.

"It's two things, actually," Roy began, clicking on something on his laptop. "First, I'm going to play you a recording. Tell me if you recognize anything."

Lou and Noah waited, listening.

Roy clicked play, and a stream of chatter began. It sounded like a restaurant. No voices were distinct enough for Lou to pick out any one conversation at first, but then it sounded like a woman and a man having a semimuffled conversation. Just when Lou was about to ask what that was all about, the chatter stopped. It was silent for a moment, and then a weird tapping began.

"Is that the 'Happy Birthday' song?" Noah frowned, moving his head to one side so he might hear better.

Roy stopped the recording and nodded. "I've listened to it a bunch, and I think it is. I can't tell what the first part is, though."

"Where'd it come from?" Lou asked.

Stiffening, Roy looked like he might not tell them at first. After a moment, he sighed and said, "It's a video recording we found on Vicki's phone. The phone was sitting on the seat next to her in the car, so we thought she might've tried to make a final phone call or snap a picture of her attacker." He shook his head. "It was pretty sparse, save for that video, which is completely dark, so it's more like an audio recording."

Lou shook her head. "I have no idea what the recording means. Sorry."

"You said there were two things you needed our help with, though," Noah said.

Roy shifted his weight in discomfort. "Yes. The second is about Silas's alibi."

"What did Silas say? Did he have one?" Noah asked, proving that he was in a much clearer state of mind than Lou. She was glad he was there with her.

Roy blinked, running his fingers through his hair. "That's the thing. He definitely has a *story*, but…" He shook his head as he let the sentence sit there unfinished.

"What about it?" Lou asked.

"Story? You think he's lying?" Noah clarified.

"I don't know what to think, to be honest." Roy cocked an eyebrow. "It seems made up. Most of it doesn't make sense. Which is why I need your help."

Noah and Lou shared a dubious look but turned back to Roy to listen to his plan.

"I want you to ask him what he saw this afternoon. Ask him to recount as many details as he can remember," Roy explained. "I want to see how closely it matches the story he told me."

"Okay." Lou believed the man was innocent, so hearing what he had to say couldn't hurt.

Roy led them into the interrogation room, seating them with their backs to the two-way mirror where he'd be listening in on their conversation. An officer led Silas into the small room a few moments later. He seemed ragged, his bowler hat nowhere to be found, and his sparse white hair sticking out in random directions instead of combed down like normal.

"What's this all about?" Silas grumbled as his eyes flashed from Lou to Noah to the two-way mirror behind them. "I thought you were going to get me out of here."

"We are," Lou assured him. "Why'd you tell me you'd been arrested? You know he's just questioning you, right?"

Silas sulked. "Might as well arrest me. You know how *he* is," he said, obviously meaning Detective Anderson.

Lou leveled him with a serious stare. "Silas, come on. We need to hear your side of this whole thing. What did you do after you left the bookshop today?"

He flinched. "It's a long story."

"We've got time," Noah said supportively. "It's important that we hear the truth."

Silas puffed out his cheeks, holding them like that for a second before exhaling. He slumped into the chair across from them. "Okay. Where should I start?"

"When you left Whiskers and Words," Lou reiterated, "you said you were going to get revenge, or maybe it was that you would do whatever it took to make her pay. I can't remember."

"I think it was both." Silas scratched at the back of his neck. Lou was glad to see pure remorse on the older man's face as he heard his words repeated back to him.

"That doesn't sound great, Silas." Noah grimaced.

"I know that *now*." Silas crossed his arms. "Okay, well, once we saw the *BSB* post about someone catching her sneaking around the bank, I stormed off in that direction."

"How long did it take you to get there?" Lou asked. It had taken her seven minutes to get from the bookshop to the bank earlier, but that had been running. Silas had been walking fast, urged on by his anger, but timing could make all the difference.

"A lot longer than it used to, I can tell you that." He patted his right knee. "The old joints don't seem to want to help me move at anything considered a quick pace." He squinted one eye. "Adam drove by in the mail truck just as I was rounding the corner of Thimble and Linen."

The local mailman was like clockwork. He always arrived at the shop at four each day, and today had been no exception. Calculating what that meant, she said, "So it was probably just after four thirty."

Silas nodded. "And at first, I didn't see anything.

Thought the *BSB* was trying to rile us up over nothing. I walked all around the block trying to find her. That was when I noticed the small trail leading into the woods behind the bank. When I checked it out, I found her car. But she wasn't there. They won't believe me because apparently, my prints are all over the thing."

Not to mention the coin you dropped nearby, Lou thought, though she kept that to herself.

"You touched the car?" Noah asked.

"I know it was wrong," Silas said. "But I didn't think it would become a crime scene. It was just her car, parked in the woods. She had a pillow and blankets in the back, like she'd been sleeping in the back seat."

"Did you open the door?" Lou asked, knowing one of the other pieces of evidence against him was a mono-grammed handkerchief.

He winced. "I did. I searched the car to make sure she wasn't keeping a bunch of money in there." From the way his face turned red, it wasn't his finest moment, and there hadn't been any such cash lying around. "It was just clothes and the blankets I mentioned. By the time I came out of the woods, I was about to give up. My knee was killing me, and my anger had kinda worn off at that point. But then I saw something crazy over by the bank."

"Crazy?" Noah asked.

"Yeah," Silas confirmed. "A person in a beekeeper suit was driving by in a car. It caught my eye, so I rounded the building to get a better look, and there she was."

"Wearing a beekeeping suit?" Lou asked in confusion.

"No. She had on a white T-shirt and jean shorts," Silas scoffed as if that were obvious.

Then what had the beekeeper suit been about? Lou wondered. She could tell Noah had similar questions as he fidgeted next to her. Lou was starting to see what Roy had been talking about. This story was feeling very disjointed and odd.

"And so you confronted her?" Noah asked, obviously moving past the beekeeper-suit comment as well.

"No," Silas snorted. "I followed her. The woman was being really weird. She was getting up real close to the bank building and pressing her ear up to the bricks like she was listening for it to tell her a secret."

"Do you think she was trying to break into the bank?" Lou asked. She knew they closed at four each weekday and at one on weekends. So it would've been closed by the time of Silas's story.

Silas let out a thin laugh. "If she was, she's terrible at it. She did the listening thing, then kicked at the wall. The woman circled the building, doing the same thing three times. Seemed more like a ritual than anything else. The last time she started talking to the plants and scratched at the earth. I thought she'd do another three turns doing that, but when I came around behind her, she was gone."

"Gone?" Noah and Lou asked together.

"She'd scooted down the alley next to Allen Kettle's house and was looking over her shoulder like she knew I was there." Silas shook his head as if gearing up for the next thing he was about to say. "Then she disappeared."

Lou blinked.

Noah's lips parted.

"I'm sorry. Disappeared?" Lou asked through a cough.

"Yeah. Vanished," Silas said. "She was there one

moment, then she was gone. I checked the alleyway three times before I left. There was no way out. I'm not sure how she did it."

"Did you go back to the car?" Noah asked.

Silas shook his head. "I was too tired at that point, and my knee was killing me. So I went home. The front desk can show you I was back at Button House by five, taking a painkiller."

Lou narrowed her eyes. That meant the medical examiner had likely placed her time of death before that, if Silas was still a suspect. Five thirty had been right about when Lou had found the body. She placed a hand on Noah's arm. "Would you mind staying here with Silas while I talk to the detective?"

He nodded, and she left the room, only waiting out in the hallway with the officer stationed there for a moment before Roy came out of the room next door.

"See?" he asked. "It doesn't make sense."

She couldn't argue with him there. "Was it the same as what he told you earlier, though?"

"Exactly." Roy scratched at his jaw.

Lou exhaled. She was tired, which meant Silas had to be absolutely beat. "Is he able to leave?"

At that, Roy winced.

"He can't?" Lou's heart dropped. She really didn't want to have to leave Silas behind.

"He can … but the captain is going to want to hear my list of suspects soon for a case this big." Roy squared his shoulders. "Once I explain everything we have on Silas, he's going to wonder why I didn't get a warrant for his arrest."

"Everything?" Lou asked, swallowing her worst fears.

"The threats, eyewitnesses seeing him following her just before you found her dead, the fingerprints all over the car, his coin, and the monogrammed handkerchief, proving he opened the door, and then the fact that she was strangled by someone with very large hands."

Lou gulped, her fingers touching her own throat as she thought. She had often marveled at Silas's huge, meaty hands. She knew he'd worked a lot of manual labor jobs when he was younger. It seemed like they'd only grown since then.

"How much time do you think you've got before the captain will pressure you for an arrest?" Lou chewed on her lip as she waited for his answer.

Roy shook his head. "A week, at the most. Probably more like five days."

"I'm going to do my best to keep him out of trouble until then," Lou said. "You look into whoever else you can."

Roy agreed and led her back to the room.

When she reentered the interrogation room, the truth must've been written all over Lou's features because Silas slumped forward and said, "They're not going to let me leave, are they?"

"Of course they will," Lou told him. "But you need to stay at Button House. No trips around town."

Noah added, "And make sure you're always where one of the security cameras or staff members can see you until Roy figures this out. Okay?"

The old man drew in a breath and let it settle. "Okay. I promise."

Together, the three of them walked out of the interrogation room and left the police station behind.

And even though Silas could leave with her tonight, she worried the next time they brought him in, he might not be so lucky. Which meant she needed to help Roy solve this case as soon as possible.

CHAPTER 5

Noah dropped off Silas at Button House before he stopped at Whiskers and Words. The sun had finally set, reminding Lou that it had only been one day since they'd seen that post on the *BSB* blog, not multiple like it seemed in her mind.

"Thank you," Lou said, the words equally full of gratitude and fatigue. The problems that had accumulated as the day had progressed weighed down on her shoulders.

"Anytime. Let me know if I can help in any other way." His eyes met hers in the dark interior of his truck.

Lou's stomach flipped with indecision. She wanted to stay there with Noah. Just being in his presence made everything feel easier. Normally, she might invite him inside or suggest that they go somewhere for a drink to debrief about their day. But her pesky crush on him was making that harder. It made her unable to be near him without thinking of what might happen if she told him the truth about her feelings.

Deciding it was one thing too many today, she reached

for the door handle and slid out of the truck, saying, "I will. Good night."

Once she slipped inside the bookshop, Lou flicked the lights on and off as she locked the door behind her, letting Noah know she was safely inside. He flashed his truck lights at her and then backed up, heading home himself.

But the moment she set down her purse, she knew this wouldn't be a relaxing evening after all. Catticus Finch was limping.

She sent Noah a quick text.

> On second thought, would you come back? Catticus is limping. If you have time to check him out, I would really appreciate it.

He sent a thumbs-up emoji in response and pulled back into the spot in front of the bookstore a few minutes later. A frown marred his features as he stepped inside, studying the cat as he walked gingerly on his front left paw.

"What'd you do, you little daredevil?" Noah knelt next to the gray tabby, scooping him into his arms and setting him on the table so he could use it as a makeshift exam space.

Focusing on the leg he wouldn't put weight on, Noah eased his fingers down the arm, applying a small amount of pressure as he went. About halfway down, Catticus flinched and pulled away, letting out a small meow of complaint.

"It's okay," Noah cooed to the cat, narrowing his eyes as he zeroed in on the paw. He spread Catticus's paw wide, forcing the claws to extend. Clicking his tongue, he held it out for Lou to look. "He's got a ripped claw and soreness extending up through his leg." Noah let the paw go, scratching the cat behind the ears. "I'd say he probably snagged it on something while he was jumping and couldn't get it unstuck, so it tore and strained a ligament."

Lou glanced up at the security camera she had for the shop after hours. Her phone had buzzed with a few notifications while she'd been at the police station, but she hadn't paid attention to the alerts, knowing she'd left the cats in the bookshop in her haste to help Silas. The camera had likely captured whatever had happened.

After a quick check of the alerts on her phone, one of which had most definitely caught the stunt, they were able to confirm that Noah had guessed correctly. Lou inhaled sharply as she watched the footage playback, covering her mouth in horror as the gray cat flinched with pain as he hung from the bookshelf for a moment before falling.

"Oh, buddy." She gently scooped Catticus into her arms and hugged him to her as he purred. "Is there an easy fix?" she asked Noah.

"I can prescribe an anti-inflammatory for the pain to make him more comfortable, but he'll heal well enough on his own as long as he stays off the leg." Noah pointed to the cat, giving him the orders instead of Lou, knowing it would be more about whether Catticus stayed out of trouble. "The pain meds will also make him a little drowsy, which will be good. Maybe he'll be less inclined to continue his parkour tendencies," Noah said, mentioning the wild sport that was all about running, jumping, and flipping off everyday items.

"That would be nice." Lou exhaled out a laugh, placing

the back of her hand on her forehead. As upsetting as this was, she knew it could've been much worse. "I can keep him upstairs during the day. The furniture isn't as tall and tempting up there."

Noah petted the contented cat in Lou's arms. "That's a great idea. I can call that prescription in right now so you can grab it tonight."

Placing a kiss on the cat's head, Lou said, "Thank you. You have no idea how much better I feel now that you came over. You're amazing."

The last sentence just kind of spilled out of her. Heat flooded her face, and her gaze cut up to catch his reaction. His brown eyes met hers, flustering her even more.

"I mean, with the cats," she blurted, then added, "and everything else. You make any situation better."

Stop talking now, Lou scolded herself, wondering if she was going to have to physically clamp her lips shut. In her attempt to make things less awkward, she'd gone and added to the discomfort.

Noah's mouth pulled up on one side, causing just one of his dimples to show. "And here I thought that was you."

Her heart soared at his compliment, but she almost couldn't appreciate the feeling because her heart was simultaneously beating way too fast in her mortification that she'd said any of that aloud. As if her racing heart was making Catticus uncomfortable, he writhed to get free, so she gently placed him on the floor at her feet. He limped off to sit next to Anne Mice who'd curled onto one of the fleece beds littered throughout the shop for the cats.

Arms free, Lou tucked a lock of hair behind her ear, and

regarded Noah. "That's very nice of you to say. Thank you."

Noah grinned down at her. "It's the truth. Did you see Silas settle when he saw you at the police station today? He was visibly calmer once he knew you were there to help him."

Lou hadn't recognized the change in the older man, only able to focus on his disgruntled body language.

Taking her bewildered expression as an answer that she hadn't, he continued on, saying, "I've never met someone who became such an important member of this community so quickly. You've been here less than two years, and none of us can imagine Button without you."

Tears gathered in the corners of Lou's eyes at the praise. "Me?" She'd always felt like it had been the kind people of Button, making the move easy on her because they felt sorry for the reason she'd moved there in the first place. "I-I didn't do anything special."

"Exactly," Noah said. "I've lived here all my life, and let me tell you, that doesn't happen often. Everyone around here adores you, Lou." Now both dimples were visible as his half smile turned into a full one.

She stared up at him, wondering if he wanted to kiss her as badly as she wanted to kiss him. But before she could say, or do, anything, a low, loud meow cut through the bookshop. Sapphire, Lou's white cat, strutted into the space. He blinked his deep-blue eyes at her.

While he was normally a quiet cat, if he was hungry, he was the loudest cat she'd ever met, not having the benefit of hearing himself since he was deaf. As if he'd broken the tension in the room, Lou and Noah broke out into laughter at the sheer volume of his feline communication skills.

"It *is* past their dinnertime," Lou said, checking her watch.

Noah cleared his throat. "Right. I'll call in that prescription so you can pick it up tonight."

"Thank you." She tried to hold his gaze, partially so he would know how much she truly appreciated his help and partly so she might see if there was a hint of whatever she'd felt pass between them still lingering behind his eyes, but Sapphire let out another long meow.

"Have a good night, Lou." Noah headed for the door.

Lou mirrored the gesture, though she stayed put, watching him leave. "You too, Noah. I'll see you tomorrow." She swallowed as he left.

Once she'd ferried Catticus upstairs—the rest of the tiny herd of cats at her heels—and had fed them, she had her car keys in hand, ready to leave for the pharmacy. Her phone rang. She was surprised to see Willow's name on the screen.

"Hey, is everything okay?" Lou answered quickly, squeezing her keys into her palm. Willow may have been a couple of hours away, but Lou was ready to go wherever she needed, however quickly.

Willow's light laugh spilled through the phone. "What? I'm not allowed to miss my best friend while I'm on vacation?" she asked.

Lou's tense body relaxed, and she sank into one of the chairs around her dining table. "I mean, sure. I just expected you to be completely caught up in your amazing plans."

Willow had gone on *at length* about how much there was to do in the small valley town.

"Touché," she said. "It is adorable here. We went on another long trail ride, took a white water rafting trip today, and then had dinner at the cutest brewery. Everything looks like a candy box here."

"That's saying something, coming from Button." Lou clicked her tongue, impressed. Button was the cutest town she'd ever been to.

"Omigosh, and Easton bought some art from this local artist. Her mountain landscape watercolors were amazing. And she told us all about her best friend's jam shop down the road," Willow gushed. "It was closed by the time we finished our rafting trip today, but we're going to hit it tomorrow before we do another trail ride."

Lou loved to hear the happiness in her friend's tone. Which was why she was a little hesitant as Willow asked how everything was going back home. Lou didn't want to sour her friend's mood, but she also wasn't good at lying, especially not to Willow.

"Well, things got dicey today," she admitted. "Vicki Younger came back to town."

Willow gasped. "She *didn't*."

Thankfully, Willow hadn't invested anything into Vicki's scheme, either, having just put most of her savings into opening her dream nursery.

"She sure did." Lou grimaced as she said the words.

Willow's reply spilled out quickly with excitement. "Did she have answers about the investments or why she's been missing for almost a month?"

Pulling in a deep breath, Lou said, "If she did, we're not

going to get them. I was on a run this evening and found her in her car in the woods. Someone had strangled her."

There was silence on the other end of the call for a beat longer than Lou expected.

"Sorry, I was putting you on speakerphone so Easton could hear," Willow explained. "That's awful. I mean, not surprising given what she did to everyone, but still awful."

"The most surprising part is that Silas is the prime suspect." Lou paused to let Willow react and then explained about the older man's threats, how he'd been following Vicki, and the overwhelming evidence pointing to him.

"What's he going to do?" Willow asked.

Lou pinched the bridge of her nose. "Roy said he should be able to buy some time before he has to make an arrest, but we just have to figure it out before then."

"Hey, Lou," Easton's deep voice cut through the line. "Is Roy being...?" Easton left the sentence hanging, knowing Lou would understand what he didn't want to say.

Lou shook her head, even though they couldn't see her. "Actually, he's like night and day from the last case." The detective had a tendency to jump to conclusions when it came to suspects and would do his best to prove himself right instead of following all the clues. "He said the evidence against Silas is stacked really high, though."

Easton sighed. "Okay, that's understandable."

"But don't you two worry. We'll figure it out," Lou assured them.

"Oh, we know *you* will," Willow said. "What else is going on?"

Lou spent the next few minutes filling in Willow about

the screen doors and then explaining what had happened with Catticus and his strained ligament.

"That makes sense," Willow said.

"That the cat hurt himself?" Lou narrowed her eyes in suspicion.

Willow chuckled. "No. It's just you sounded upset, maybe even a little flustered. More than just about Silas."

Lou grinned. Of course her best friend would've been able to tell that, even through the phone. "I mean, yeah. It's Catticus and Silas, but mostly it's Noah. There's something between us, but I don't know how to move forward."

Easton cleared his throat, and Lou realized her mistake.

"I'm still on speakerphone, aren't I?" She closed her eyes out of embarrassment.

"I'm so sorry," Willow blurted. "I didn't realize you would—"

"It's not your fault," Lou said, interrupting Willow's apology. "I forgot."

"If it's any consolation, I already knew." Easton's voice came tentatively from the background. "Not because Willow told me or anything," he rushed to add. "It's just, the two of you have always seemed like a good match, and you get along so well."

"I promise I didn't tell him," Willow reiterated.

"She didn't," Easton added.

Lou laughed. "Don't worry. I get it. Plus, you two are together now. I wouldn't be upset if you had, Willow."

"Did something happen between the two of you?" Willow asked. "Do you want to talk about it?"

"No. Nothing happened. I just keep wondering if something should. But I should probably go to the pharmacy before it closes, to get the medication for Catticus." Lou sighed. "Hearing that Easton noticed something between us *does* help, though. I know it's not just in my head, you know?"

"See?" Easton said in a way that told Lou that Willow had sent him a scolding look for butting in before.

Lou chuckled. "Thanks for the call. Have fun tomorrow, you two."

"Good luck with the start of quilt craziness," Willow said, before saying a last farewell and hanging up.

Right. With everything else going on, Lou had almost forgotten that the quilting convention began the next day. Willow was unapologetic about her negative feelings about the thing, citing that it was always during the *already packed* last week of the school year, and *couldn't they wait one extra week?* Willow was one of the few locals who'd been ecstatic when it had been cancelled last year.

Lou thought she might feel differently now that she was a business owner. Apparently, it was a great boost for local shops. Lou had stocked extra quilting books, magazines, and knickknacks for the week, setting up a table near the front of the store with all the quilt-specific offerings. But she was glad Willow had been able to get away. Peggy Lee and Beau could handle the nursery for the week.

Off the phone, Lou grabbed her keys, ready to leave for the pharmacy. As much as she wanted to attempt to change Willow's mind about the quilting convention, it just seemed like one more thing on her already full plate.

CHAPTER 6

The next day, the town was abuzz. Not only had the quilting convention kicked off that morning with a list of offered classes and tutorials, but everyone who entered Whiskers and Words had also heard of Silas's place at the top of the suspect list in Vicki Younger's murder, thanks to a new post on the *Behind the Scenes Button* blog.

As much as Lou missed Silas that morning, she was glad he'd heeded her warning and stayed home. Not only would it help keep him out of trouble, but he also would've gotten quickly fed up with every other customer asking questions about what had happened to Vicki.

It wasn't just Silas who wasn't there, however. None of Lou's regulars stopped by that day. She hoped everything was okay with them, especially George, whom she'd yet to check in with about the date she'd been on.

Lou meant to text George, but between cleaning up from the book swap the day before, fielding questions from locals, and running upstairs to check on Catticus whenever she could, Lou barely had a moment to drink a glass of water from the time she opened until she closed that evening. Once she turned the Open sign to the other side, all she wanted to do was make herself a pitcher of iced tea, open all the windows in her apartment, and sit on the couch with a book.

Instead, she headed to the quilting convention. She'd promised Noah, and she *was* interested in meeting his famous Aunt Cricket she'd heard so much about yesterday.

Lou drove out to Button Memorial Park, noting that the large parking lot was still nearly full even though the event closed within the hour. She wasn't surprised, having seen the flyers about extra parking in the grocery store lot, and Martie, the town rideshare driver, advertising half-priced rides from the hospital parking lot, which always had more than enough spaces. Feeling rather lucky, she pulled into one of the last spots and got out, reveling in the breeze wafting through the park.

The wind fluttered through the large white tent and sent the ducklings, who'd grown quite a bit in the last few months, quacking in the park's duck pond. It was a lovely day: the breeze making similar temperatures from yesterday feel manageable, especially once she was under the cover of the large white tent.

Inside, there were vendor booths set up along the exterior walls of the tent and a space for classes, lectures, and tutorials in the middle. At the moment, it looked like Noah's grandmother was finishing up teaching a class on machine embroidery, based on the sign sitting on an easel near the tables full of sewing machines, with people diligently working while she came around to check their work.

Lou didn't have any interest in joining the class, but she wandered along the edge of the tent, perusing the vendor tables. She scanned for Noah, shopping as she searched.

There were people selling beautiful fabrics, intricate quilt block patterns, specialty quilting machines, and there were also finished quilts for sale. Lou wondered if she should pick up a nice quilt for her bed. She could just picture one of the floral designs draped over her mattress, the sun shining through the window onto the cats who would inevitably curl up on it.

Before she could decide on one, she heard her name.

"Louisa Henry? Lou, darling." A woman beckoned to her from behind a booth selling antique buttons. She grinned the moment Lou turned toward her. "It *is* you. I feel like I'd know you anywhere based on the way Noah described you."

And while Lou had never seen the woman before, she immediately knew who she was.

"Cricket." Lou rushed over, allowing the woman to pull her into a tight hug. "It's so nice to meet you. How's it going?" Lou asked. From the crowds, it seemed like the convention was already a hit.

But Cricket's face didn't match that assumption. Her eyes swiveled back and forth, and she leaned forward. "Let's just say this convention isn't the only thing that is *in tents*." She widened her big brown eyes. "Get it? *Intense?*"

Despite Cricket's punny joke, Lou didn't feel like laughing. "What? Why?" Lou worried for a moment that the *BSB*'s very first post about Rosa Ramero's dire financial situation might've been true after all. She scooted behind

Cricket's booth, and they had a seat. She immediately felt like she'd known the woman for not just years, but decades.

"The higher-ups are *not* happy," Cricket whispered out of the corner of her mouth as she smiled at a group of customers who slowed down to peruse her booth.

"Higher-ups, like Noah's family?" Lou asked quietly.

Cricket shook her head. "The sponsors."

Lou didn't know enough about sewing or quilts to recognize the names of the trifecta of businesses everyone listed off each time someone mentioned the sponsors, but she knew they paid for the tent rental, supplies, and advertisements for the event. Based on the way everyone involved cowered before them and seemed to worship the ground they walked on, Lou figured they were a pretty big deal.

"What are they unhappy about?" Lou asked.

Maybe the *BSB* had been right. There were financial troubles, just not with the Ramero family.

Cricket's gaze swung right and left. "They're still bitter about last year, and now Button's the scene of a fresh murder. There have been more than a few rumblings that they don't think Button is the best place to continue putting their money. They're talking about either pulling their funding for next year or even trying to take the event to another town, closer to the big city."

"They can't do that, though. Can they?" Lou realized she didn't know that much about the event. "I thought the Rameros started the convention decades ago."

"They did," Cricket said. "But they can't trademark an event, and after helping them run this for years, what's stopping the investors from hiring someone else to put on their own?"

Worry rumbled in Lou's thoughts for a few minutes while Cricket helped a customer.

"Anyway," Cricket said, turning to face Lou after the customer had paid and left. "There's more than one good reason to want this whole murder case to get wrapped up as soon as possible. It's got the Rameros so worked up, they've got Noah manning the quilt shop while Paloma works her magic with the classes. She's amazing, but she tires a lot more quickly than she used to," Cricket explained, jabbing a thumb over to where Noah's grand-mother was wrapping up her class. "Usually, Paloma stays behind, but this is an all-hands-on-deck event."

As if helping Silas avoid prison wasn't a good enough reason to find the true killer, this was yet another worthy cause. "I wondered where Noah was," Lou said.

"He was adamant I find you right away. He didn't want you to worry." Cricket shot Lou a sidelong glance. "So, tell me. What's going on between the two of you?"

Face growing hot, Lou couldn't seem to meet Cricket's gaze. "Between us?" Lou laughed awkwardly. "Me and Noah?" she asked, feigning ignorance.

But Cricket wasn't Noah's fake aunt for nothing. She placed a hand on her hip and tilted her head toward Lou. "Honey, I haven't heard him talk about anyone so much, except Marigold, of course. That man thinks the world of you, and based on the color rushing to your cheeks, I'd say you feel the same about him."

Lou swallowed, glancing around as if Noah might show up at any moment. "It's … complicated."

Cricket placed a hand on Lou's shoulder, patting it twice. "He told me about your husband." She held put both hands in front of her. "I'm not trying to rush you. Goodness knows you need time to heal and everyone moves at their own pace. I just would hate to see you hold back if you're ready." She winked at Lou.

"Thank you." Lou smiled. Even though she'd just met this woman, she felt comfortable confiding in her, as if she'd been a trusted confidant for years. "I think it might be time to tell him how I feel." Saying it out loud lifted a weight off Lou's chest.

Cricket beamed. "Speaking of Noah. I was supposed to bring him dinner over at the quilt shop. Rosa wants to keep it open late in case people head over there after the convention shuts down for the evening, but it looks like I've got a line here." Cricket motioned to the customers wandering by her booth. "Would you be so kind as to bring him something?" She fished a twenty out of her purse and shoved it toward Lou.

Holding up her hand to show she couldn't take the money, Lou said, "It's my treat. I owe him." Lou smiled as she stood. "Bye, Cricket. It was great to meet you."

"Likewise. I'll come by the bookshop soon. Cats and books are two of my favorite things, so I think I'll be spending a lot of time at Whiskers and Words now that I'm back in town," Cricket called.

It sounded as if Lou might've picked up another regular, something she wasn't sad about, not one bit.

When Lou got back to her car, she pulled out her phone to text Noah and ask what he wanted for dinner, but then she remembered it was Thursday and the Thai food truck Noah loved would be parked in the hardware store's lot.

She swung by, grabbing one of each of her favorite dishes and pulled up in front of Material Girls half an hour later. Leftover Thai food was her favorite, so she always erred on the side of ordering too much. The bell on the front door dinged as Lou entered the quilt shop. She had little cause to shop there over the past year and a half, not being much of a quilter, but it had been the place where she'd first met Noah upon arriving in town.

It looked just like it had that day, holding the same themed bolts of fabric and specialty options along the walls. The same vinegary smell permeated the air, mixing with the soft cotton smell of the fabric. There were no customers at the moment, but Lou knew they might trickle in once they left the convention.

Noah stood behind the cutting counter that doubled as a checkout register. He wore the same pink apron she'd seen him wearing that very first meeting. And just like that time, his entire face seemed to light up as he saw her.

"Hey, what a surprise." His dimples deepened as his smile grew.

She held up the bags. "I brought dinner to thank you for my doors. Cricket said you might need some food."

Noah arched a dark eyebrow. "She already has you running her errands, huh?"

Lou dipped her chin. "She's already committed to spending a lot of time at the bookshop, and I think Willow has competition for my best friend spot."

"Sounds like Cricket. She could make friends with a

paper bag, but she's selective. It's a compliment that she likes you so much." Noah laughed.

A warmth spread through Lou. She'd felt special already, but it was nice to have Noah confirm it too.

"Care to join me?" Noah asked, moving aside a bolt of fabric so there was a makeshift table on the cutting counter.

"Sure." A lightness expanded through Lou's chest.

Cricket was right. She was ready to move forward. Lou opened her mouth to say more, but Noah's daughter ran over from the back room of the shop.

"Lou? When did you get here?" Marigold asked, rushing over to wrap her arms around Lou's waist in a tight hug.

Holding up the bags of Thai food as she accepted the hug, Lou said, "Just bringing your dad dinner, since Cricket couldn't get away from the tent. You hungry?"

The girl sniffed the bags, eyes wide. She was just like her father.

Lou motioned for her to join them at the cutting counter. They chatted about the convention for a few minutes in between bites, and Lou gave Noah an update on Catticus.

"How's Silas doing?" Marigold asked after swallowing a big bite of wide rice noodles.

Lou glanced at her and then at Noah, in awe.

Noah shrugged. "Word gets around fast in Button, even up to the elementary school. Goldie found out at lunch today, didn't you, Petal?"

She nodded proudly. "Penelope Reynolds was bragging about it like it was cool. I told her there's no way Silas did that."

Lou had been swallowing, and she almost choked on the bite. "Reynolds? He has a daughter?"

"Granddaughter," Noah corrected. "His son, Eric, lives in town and has a daughter who's the same age as Marigold."

Lou sighed. "I know Roy's on the case, and it feels nice to trust he'll do a thorough job, but I can't help but think about what we can do to speed up the process to help him."

"I'll be right back. I have to use the bathroom." Marigold jumped up from her seat and skipped off to the back room where the shop restroom was located.

Leaning close, Noah said, "Eric's wife has substance-abuse issues, and she's been in and out of recovery centers and the kids' lives. For the past few years, he's been raising Penelope and Luke alone."

"That's awful." Lou placed a hand over her heart.

They quieted as Marigold returned, having firsthand proof that the kids of Button gossiped just about as much as the adults, and not wanting Marigold to hear anything she shouldn't repeat about Eric Reynolds or his family.

"So, Goldie, you're almost done with school, huh?" Lou asked, wanting to change the subject to something more upbeat.

Marigold's eyes sparkled with the glimmer of summer. "Tomorrow's our last day."

"Am I getting a summer helper again?" Lou asked. "It sounds like Cricket's planning to spend some time with the cats each day now that she's back in town," she told Marigold, since she'd already shared that news with Noah.

Noah wet his lips, looking at his daughter. "Actually, Goldie's got some exciting plans."

The little girl tucked a lock of her hair behind her ear nervously. "Mom and I are leaving tomorrow for a three-week trip to Ireland to visit her ancestors."

"Well, *learn* about her ancestors and *visit* her cousins who still live there," Noah clarified.

Breaking into a huge grin, Lou said, "That's so amazing. You're going to have such a great trip."

Marigold's gaze dropped to the piece of broccoli she'd speared on the end of her fork. "I've never traveled that far away. I'm nervous. And I'm sad that I'll miss you and the cats."

"We'll still have plenty of summer left once you get back," Lou told her, placing a hand on her arm, which caused Marigold to glance up at her. "Traveling is such an amazing gift. It makes you appreciate how other cultures live at the same time as helping you appreciate your home. It's going to be fantastic." Seeing Marigold wasn't completely sold, Lou added, "Plus, there are a ton of really amazing libraries in Ireland."

At that, Marigold's pouty lips pulled into a smile. "Really?" She looked at her dad.

Noah nodded. "With very old books. You'll love it."

"I'll take a lot of pictures for you, Lou." Marigold started eating again, apparently over her fears for now.

Lou beamed. "I would love that." She was about to take another bite of her curry when she got the sensation that someone was staring at her. Glancing up, she noticed Noah's eyes were locked on to her. He stared at her almost as hungrily as he had when she'd first brought out the Thai food.

Clearing his throat, Noah turned back to his meal.

"Did you hear the *BSB* said the quilt convention is going to bring twice as many people this year as last year?" Marigold asked.

Lou stopped chewing midbite in her surprise. She swallowed and said, "You read the town blog?"

Marigold shook her head. "No, but everyone's moms and dads do, so we talk about it at school all the time. I'm just happy they're posting nice stuff about grandma now," she said, referencing that first *BSB* post speculating about Rosa's financial situation.

Lou and Noah shared an amused smirk at the girl's confidence and then went back to eating. Just as Lou had suspected, customers began filtering into the shop a short while later, so Lou helped Marigold clean up the leftovers while Noah helped the customers.

After saying goodbye to Marigold, Lou slipped out the front door while Noah was cutting fabric for an older woman, telling herself that she didn't want to distract him when he had to work. The pit in her stomach reminded her that it was something else entirely, and she resolved to have a candid chat with the man as soon as she got the chance.

But with the murder investigation and an injured cat to look after on her end, and this quilting convention on his, Lou wasn't sure when exactly that would be.

CHAPTER 7

That evening, once Lou was home and snuggled onto the couch with the cats, she pulled out her laptop instead of the book she was reading, and she did something she hadn't done for months.

She visited the website for the *Behind the Scenes in Button* blog.

If she had any hope of figuring out who actually killed Vicki, she had a feeling she was going to need information from the gossipy site. Wincing at the glaring lemon-lime color of the website background, Lou focused on the list of post titles and the days they'd been published.

She zeroed in on a post entitled "Miracle Serum?" from the previous month, and she clicked on it.

As any Buttonite who's in the know is already aware, Vicki Younger, a new resident of Brine, is offering an investment opportunity. Snail Serum X is an anti-aging product taking our town by storm. I know that sounds too good to be true, but this writer can tell you from experience that the stuff lives up to the hype. I won't divulge my age, since you don't even know my name, but let's just say I've got a few wrinkles. After just a week of using the serum, I saw a marked improvement in the suppleness of my skin and a reduction in the wrinkles. Early adopters are plenty, but get in quick because the company's sure to be big, and shares are going fast. You can talk to Silas Owings, Eric Reynolds, Jane Clarke, or Chad Smalley, who are all early investors, if you'd like to know about how to get involved.

Lou's eyes narrowed at the name. Eric Reynolds. Marigold had just been talking about Penelope, Eric's daughter. But the more important distinction was the one Noah made when Marigold had gone to the bathroom, about Eric being a single father and having fallen on hard times. How could he be one of the investors if he was struggling financially?

Needing to know more, Lou searched the blog for any other mention of the man. When she couldn't find any, she closed her laptop. Normally, she would've called Willow, hoping Easton would be close by to help fill in the blanks Willow might not know because she hadn't lived in Button her whole life, like her detective boyfriend. But Lou wasn't about to interrupt their getaway. She gulped as she realized there was someone else she could call on.

Noah.

The devastatingly handsome look he'd given her at dinner that evening, the one that felt unsettling in the best and most terrifying way, gave her pause. But hadn't she gone there that evening to tell him the truth about how she felt? Marigold's presence had been what stopped her. So a look like the one he'd given her should make her feel excited, not scared—in theory. She almost checked her watch to make sure it was late enough that the quilt shop would be closed. But a quick glance out her window told her she'd spent more time than she'd realized looking through the *BSB* blog. The sun had already set while she was snooping.

Pulling out her phone, Lou texted Noah before she could chicken out.

Do you have Goldie tonight?

Sure, it may sound like a silly question since she'd just been with Noah and Marigold earlier. But Noah could've been merely spending a few more hours with his daughter before he dropped her off with Cassidy to get ready for their trip.

Lou inwardly applauded herself for being brave. Just as quickly as the feeling arrived, however, it disappeared as she reread the message she'd sent. Was it just her, or did that sound suggestive? Quickly, Lou added a second text.

I have a few questions about the Vicki
Younger case, and I'm wondering if you
can meet. Maybe the bistro?

There, she thought. *That's better. Much clearer.* The bistro stayed open for another hour and a half. They could each have a glass of wine, maybe split a dessert while they talked.

Again, the seconds that passed only proved to make her nervous about what she'd written. This time she was worried because he usually answered right away, and as she thought through the reasons he might not, she remembered how stretched thin his time was that week because of the quilting convention.

It was nine thirty on a Thursday night. He might be fast asleep, completely drained from an exhausting day, and here she was trying to leech information out of him about their neighbors in town.

She was about to add another text to clarify that it didn't need to be tonight, when three bubbles appeared on his side of the texting screen, and an answer popped up.

> I do. She just got into bed. Do you want to come here?

Lou swallowed the hot feeling that crept up her throat. She wanted to go to his house so badly.

Then he added,

> I don't have fancy desserts, but I have wine.

Embarrassment flushed over her. Had her suggestion of wine made her sound presumptuous? She shot back a clarifying text.

> We don't have to drink. The bistro's just the only thing open tonight. I'll be right over, if you don't mind.

The fact that she could call him wasn't lost on her. She wondered if Noah had thought about that too. But he'd been the one to invite her over, so maybe he didn't care either.

See you in a few.

Butterflies danced in her stomach. Oh, who was she kidding? Her insides were a jumble, bad enough that it was beyond fluttering insects. No, what she had was a whole swarm of large bats, flapping and somersaulting all over the place.

She thought about changing into something a little nicer than the tank top she'd had on earlier, but that might make her seem like she was trying too hard. So she stayed in the same clothes, grabbing a cardigan off the back of the chair in her bedroom before she left. Heading out the door before she could change her mind, Lou drove to Noah's house.

He lived in a small gray cottage in a neighborhood on Pattern Drive. His truck was parked in the driveway when she pulled up, and he opened the door. Lou pulled in a deep breath, counted to five, and then exhaled slowly. Fortified, she climbed out of the car and walked up to his front door, heart hammering so loudly in her ears, she could barely hear her footsteps against the concrete pathway.

Instead of opening the door wider and stepping back to let her inside, Noah came out onto the covered porch and pulled the door shut behind him. So ... maybe he *didn't* want her coming inside. And maybe she'd completely misread his look earlier.

"It's such a nice night. I thought we could sit out here." He gestured to two chairs to his right. A small table sat in between them. He'd already poured two glasses of red wine for them.

"It is really lovely." Lou rubbed her hands up and down her arms, glad she'd brought the cardigan.

Following his lead, she sat in the chair closest to her. He settled into the other. Picking up his glass of wine, he clinked it against hers.

"So, what did you want to ask me?" Noah asked.

Lou couldn't be sure, but she thought she heard a hint of a smirk behind his question, as if he, too, thought her interest in the case was simply a ruse to come over.

Ready to prove him wrong, Lou said, "Earlier, when Goldie mentioned Penelope and her dad, Eric, you said he was a single dad and was having a rough go of it. You meant financially, right?"

Noah blinked, as if surprised that Lou actually had a question. "Uh, yeah. I mean, it's none of my business, but Goldie talks about how Penelope gets free lunches at school, which usually means they need financial assistance."

"I won't spread that around," Lou assured him, holding up a hand to stop his worries. "But I noticed his name was listed on the *BSB* blog under the investors in Vicki's serum scheme. That just doesn't seem to fit unless he recently came into money."

Noah sipped at his wine. "Not that I know of. In fact, I think Goldie mentioned Penelope was having a chat with their teacher the other day because there was a fine for a library book she hadn't brought back, and she was in tears because she looked everywhere in their house and couldn't find it. The librarian told her not to worry about it, but that doesn't sound like the daughter of someone who's just come into enough money to invest."

Lou tapped her fingernails against the wineglass as she sipped and contemplated that. "What if he invested their savings, all they had? That might make him desperate."

"Enough to kill?" Noah asked, apparently seeing where Lou was going. "I guess. It seems like a terrible idea. I mean, his dad is a Button police officer, even if he does mostly just run the phones now."

"Maybe Eric was at his wits' end, and Vicki sounded like she could finally help him see the light at the end of his money-trouble tunnel." Lou sat forward. "We all heard her pitch. She promised that the company would be huge, that the shares would be worth so much more than the measly ten grand we would pay for them. It seemed like a sure thing when she talked about it."

Averse as Lou was to talking investments, even she'd been tempted. Silas had mentioned that Lou was never interested in investing, but he'd been wrong about that. Internally, she'd struggled with the idea of passing up something that seemed so smart. She didn't want to be one of those foolish people who had the opportunity to buy stock in a multi-million-dollar company at its inception and decided not to. And those insecure thoughts came from the mind of someone who had a large amount of savings. She couldn't imagine how tempting the idea might be if someone felt like they were drowning, and this might finally be the lifeline they'd been waiting for.

Noah took another long sip of his wine. "Now that you mention it, I can't help but consider the location of Eric's house."

"Where's that?" Lou asked, almost choking on a sip of wine. The excited gasp almost made her breathe the liquid instead of drinking it.

"On the other side of the woods, where you found her car." Noah clicked his tongue.

Lou felt her fingers tremble with the excitement of a lead. "Maybe he saw her come back into town, and he went to get revenge."

"Or simply to get his investment back." Noah shrugged.

Armed with the information she needed to dig more into Eric Reynolds as a suspect, Lou could've left, but the night was clear and warm, and it was rather nice sitting on the porch with Noah.

"How are you feeling about Marigold being gone for three weeks?" she asked, changing the subject. "Was it a quick decision?" Lou added, having been surprised that she had heard nothing about the trip before tonight, the day before they would have to leave town.

"Not exactly," Noah said. "Cass and I have been talking about it for a while, but Goldie gets anxious if she has time to build something up in her mind. We wanted her to focus on the last few weeks of school," he said. "Plus, there have been enough big changes in her life lately already."

"Like?" Lou hadn't heard of anything she would consider a *big change*.

Pulling in a deep breath, Noah said, "Cassidy started dating someone."

Lou blinked, trying to temper her surprise for Noah's sake. "Oh." *I guess the BSB doesn't know everything that happens in town*, Lou thought to herself, having seen nothing of the sort on the gossip site. "Is this the first person she's seen since you two divorced?"

"No." Noah ran a hand down his face, stopping to rub at his eyes in a way that spoke to his long day. "And it's not like I still have feelings for her, in that way; it's just … it's an adjustment. We disagreed on how quickly Cass introduced him to Marigold, but she said they're serious." Noah shrugged.

Lou pressed her lips together. Noah and Cassidy were sort of the exemplary divorced couple, working together so well to keep Marigold happy and cared for that Lou had even asked Willow why they'd gotten divorced in the first place if they were such a good team. Willow had explained that they hadn't been that good together as a couple, and that Cassidy had left Noah for another realtor she'd met at a conference. And even though Cassidy and that man were no longer together, Noah and Cassidy's divorce had stuck.

Still, hearing that Cassidy had introduced Marigold to a boyfriend was a surprise to Lou. From what Lou had seen, Cassidy was usually more careful about making sure she and Noah were on the same page.

Lou's heart hurt at the myriad of emotions she could tell were going through his mind at that moment. His expression was trapped between excitement and pain. Divorce was a very hard thing, even if it was the right decision. Lou could tell he wanted to spend as much time as possible with his daughter, but he also didn't want to deny her time with her mother.

"Divorce is rough," she said in summary.

Noah's mouth pulled into a side smile, showing off one dimple in the moonlight. "It is. And it's not like I could've gone on this trip, anyway."

"She's not bringing the boyfriend, is she?" Lou asked.

"No," he said. "I just meant that this is an important

time for my family, and they need me here to help with the convention."

Lou watched him. "Sure. But it's still okay to feel like you're missing out. Just like seeing Cassidy dating someone is tough, even if you don't still have feelings for her."

He caught Lou's gaze and nodded.

"Is he the first new partner Marigold has met?" Lou asked. "Have *you* ever introduced her to anyone you've dated?" she clarified, getting to the heart of what she really wanted to know.

"I haven't dated anyone since we divorced. I was feeling ready and then…" Noah glanced away.

"Then what?" Lou kept herself from leaning forward or sounding too invested. Had something happened that she didn't know about?

Noah fidgeted with his wineglass. "I just had to remind myself to be patient, to give things time."

Lou's spirits flattened. That seemed like a very clear admission that he wasn't ready for a relationship. Guilt overwhelmed her. If he wasn't even ready, should she be?

It had been two years since she'd lost Ben. Sometimes that felt like forever, other days it felt like the blink of an eye. Grief was a confusing thing to navigate, especially because it looked so different for every person who experienced it. She tried not to place expectations or assign timelines to her feelings, but the idea of moving on to loving someone other than Ben was a big step. Maybe Noah was right. Patience was key when it came to getting back out there. She could give it more time.

Slightly embarrassed by her underlying reason for coming to see Noah, Lou's thoughts returned to the *real* reason she'd come over in the first place: to get more information about Eric Reynolds, and Vicki's murder. Silas and solving the case *had* to be her focus for now.

She didn't have room in her mind for relationship worries.

Setting her hands on her knees, Lou said, "Speaking of time…" She gave him as much of a smile as she could muster. "I'd better get back so I can get some sleep."

Noah stood. He walked her to the edge of the porch. "I'll stop by tomorrow to check on Catticus, if that's okay."

"See you then." Lou headed to her car, wishing her heart didn't hurt so much as she left Noah behind.

CHAPTER 8

Thoughts of Eric Reynolds and his desperation grew inside Lou's imagination that night while she slept, and by the time she awoke, she couldn't wait to get the local gossip about the man and find out if the people who'd known him the longest thought he might be capable of murder.

Lou had to admit that the *BSB* blog had helped her with the initial information, but she was biased because she felt like she had the best local info right there in the bookshop. Even with Silas staying home for a while, George and Forrest usually supplied her with sympathetic and rational views on anything she wanted to know about the town or the people in it. She knew she wouldn't get sensationalized stories either. That was the best thing. Even if George sometimes blew things out of proportion, Forrest would calmly bring it back into focus with his empathetic lens.

She just hoped they would show up today. Yesterday being a day without any of her regulars had been harder than she thought it would be. When Lou opened the bookshop to three people instead of just the two she'd been expecting, she was ecstatic. It might not have been Silas standing out front with George and Forrest, but seeing Cricket there was the next best thing.

"Sorry we didn't make it yesterday," George said as she walked past her into the shop.

Unlike the other day, her cat Geralt was with her, strapped to her in a baby carrier and happy as could be. It had been shocking to see at first, but now the sight was as normal as seeing someone walking their dog down the street.

George perched on the edge of the loveseat. "Forrest and I decided to split our time since we heard about Silas. We went and visited him at Button House yesterday, knowing he'd be going stir crazy, and *you* get us today." She held her hands flat under her chin and smiled sweetly, like she was posing for a picture.

"Oh good," Lou said. "How is Silas doing?"

"He's okay." Forrest dipped his head in greeting as he walked inside.

George scoffed. "He is *not*. The guy's worried out of his mind and more irritable than usual."

"Like I said, *okay* … given the circumstances," Forrest said, arching an eyebrow toward George. "I don't think any of us is our best self when we're accused of something like that."

Lou agreed. "And what a lovely surprise it is to see you," Lou said, ushering Cricket inside next.

"I told you I'd have to come by," the older woman said, pulling Lou into a tight side hug and planting a kiss on her cheek like they were old, dear friends.

"I didn't think I'd be so lucky as to get a visit this soon, though." Lou stepped back, making sure the screen door latched behind them. "Who's at your booth?"

Cricket waved a hand in the air. "I just put up a sign saying I'd be back later. Who needs to buy buttons this early in the morning? Plus, I had to come by and see if you had any developments to report." Cricket settled onto the love seat, patting it as if demanding Lou sit with her.

Forrest pretended to not be interested as he opened his paperback and started petting Anne Mice, but George made no such efforts.

"Developments in what? Are you trying to figure out who killed Vicki?" She settled onto the arm of the couch next to Cricket. Geralt, who'd woken up at his owner's loud questions, extended his claws just enough that he could pick at the corner of Cricket's sleeve. "Hey, watch it, you little stinker." George laughed, moving her body so he wouldn't be able to scratch anyone.

Cricket cleared her throat in discomfort as she realized her mistake. Loud as the woman was, she also held enough tact to gather that airing Lou's feelings about Noah was obviously not something Lou was comfortable with just yet, even around her favorite regulars.

"I am," Lou said, hating that her voice cracked around the lie. Well, it wasn't technically a lie. She was investigating the murder case. It just hadn't been what Cricket had been talking about. "And I do have a development. I saw on the *BSB* that one of Vicki's original investors was Eric Reynolds. It doesn't hurt that he lives on the other side of the woods from where she was killed. Do you think he could be capable of something like that?"

George sucked in a breath. But if Lou thought it was out of excitement about Eric as a suspect, she was sorely disappointed when George asked, "You read the *BSB* blog?" She jabbed an accusatory finger in Lou's direction. "I thought you said it was bad for the town."

Lou rolled her eyes. "Fine, yes, I read it. Only to find out who might've had a reason to want Vicki dead instead of Silas, and the *BSB* had the list of investors. I did it for Silas," she reiterated.

"It also surprised me to see Eric's name on that list," Forrest admitted, giving Lou a much-appreciated break from George's scrutiny.

"Because he's a single father?" Lou asked, then peered around to make sure no one was walking by on the sidewalk who might overhear their conversation through the new screen door. "Supporting those kids on his own?"

Forrest nodded. "And because his father was so vocal about how anyone supporting her idea was a fool."

Lou hadn't heard that, but it sounded just like Officer Reynolds. "Knowing his father would be upset with him for investing and losing the money would've been even more motivation to see if he could get it back," Lou mused.

George's eyes were wide as she asked, "What are you going to do?"

"Yeah," Cricket said. "I doubt all that's going to be enough for Detective Crabby to get an arrest warrant."

Lou frowned. "Hey, Roy's doing much better."

"He still might arrest Silas," George muttered.

"Because Silas's fingerprints were all over Vicki's car, he threatened her, was seen following her right before she died, and his monogrammed handkerchief was stuck in her car door." Lou placed a hand on her hip.

George wrinkled her nose. "Yeah, that's kind of a lot." She snapped her fingers. "If Silas was following her, maybe he caught sight of the actual killer."

A man walked by the bookshop as George was talking, stopped, and came back to read the cat adoption profiles in the window. Lou couldn't count how many customers she'd hooked by having those profiles in the window. She didn't want to stare at the man, however, so she returned to the conversation she was having with the regulars.

"Silas saw Vicki do some weird stuff, and then he said she disappeared up a driveway between two houses near the bank. I think talking to Eric is my best bet," Lou said. "I'll just start by asking where he was on Wednesday around five. Maybe he has a good alibi. He is a single dad after all. Maybe his kids were with him and can vouch for where he was."

A smile curled over Lou's lips as the man who'd been looking over the adoption profiles came inside. He nodded to Lou and the regulars before disappearing down one of the bookshop's aisles. Not wanting to get caught talking about murder in front of new customers, Lou changed the subject.

"Let's talk about something more pleasant," Lou said. "George, how was your date the other night?"

George's cheeks immediately turned a bright shade of red. "Not great. We didn't even make it to the appetizers."

"Did he do something bad?" Cricket asked, hand on her hip.

Shrugging, George said, "No, I think we could just both tell we weren't a match."

"If Gianna and I had done that, we wouldn't be married. We butted heads like nobody's business at first," Forrest said with a snort of laughter.

George squinted. "I can't imagine anyone *not* getting along with you."

Lou had to agree. Forrest was not only easygoing, but overwhelmingly kind.

"Are you sure you didn't call it too soon?" Cricket asked.

"You know what?" George stood from where she'd been perched on the arm of the couch. "You're all right. I don't know what I was thinking." She slapped a hand to her forehead. "I'm going to go give him a second chance, right now," she said in a sickly sweet voice that had no business coming out of the George they knew. "Come on, Geralt. Let's go find you a dad." And with that, she wafted out of the bookshop like a dramatic, lovesick woman from an old romance movie.

Lou, Forrest, and Cricket blinked at the front door.

"She could've just *told* us we were wrong." Lou chuckled, still surprised by George's sudden departure.

"That's a girl who knows her mind," Cricket said with a whistle.

Lou couldn't argue. George knew herself better than most people twice her age. If she was sure she and her date weren't a match, they needed to trust her instead of pushing back with stories of how they or people they knew had gone from butting heads to holding hands.

Cricket stood as well, though much slower than George

had. "Well, I should probably get back to the convention," she announced. "See you around. And Lou, let me know if you need a partner in crime solving," she added with a wink before slipping out the front door.

The man who'd been shopping around came forward clutching a book about botany. Lou was happy for the purchase but disappointed that he hadn't asked about any of the cats. He paid for his book and left.

Lou wrinkled her nose once it was just her and Forrest once more. "I think Silas might be right. Those jasmine plants are almost too fragrant with the door open." She waved a hand in front of her face.

"You're right." Forrest frowned.

Even Sapphire sniffed at the air and squinted at the intense smell. Lou closed the door for a bit to mitigate the smell, then she busied herself with unpacking a new order of books while Forrest opened his book and got in a little reading before his next client. The rest of the day plodded along. And even though day one of the convention had been a tremendous hit sales-wise for Lou, the second day was not following suit. In fact, when there was not a single customer between the hours of one and three in the afternoon, Lou started to worry.

That was when she remembered it was the last day of school.

"That's why it's so slow. People are celebrating the beginning of summer vacation," she said to the cats as they lounged in the beams of sunshine.

Remembering that she was going to search out Eric Reynolds after work that day, and that he had a daughter the same age as Marigold, she wondered if he would pick up his kids from school. That might be the perfect way to run into him and ask him about his whereabouts on Wednesday.

Plus, it's not like you're missing out on a ton of sales by closing early, she reasoned with herself. *And, this way, if he is the killer, you'll be surrounded by witnesses, and he won't be able to hurt you,* Lou added as she closed the shop early, put on running clothes, and started toward the elementary school.

The parking lot was packed, making Lou glad she'd run instead of trying to drive. Though, the sun was beating down, and it was pretty hot by the time she jogged over to where a bunch of parents waited for the children to be released from the building. She located Eric right away. He looked too much like his father for her to miss the guy.

Sidling up to him, she found him chatting with another parent about summer plans.

"We're probably just going to stick around here," Eric said. "Maybe take day trips to Silver Lake here and there."

Right, because money's especially tight for you if you lost your savings in Vicki's scam, Lou thought.

"Lou?" the other dad asked, turning to frown at her. "You don't have a kid who goes here, do you?" he asked, as if he was worried he'd missed an important piece of town gossip about one of the newer residents.

She recognized him as a parent who often brought his kids in to shop for books and smiled. "Oh, uh … no." She laughed awkwardly. "I was just jogging by and thought it would be fun to watch the kids leave school for the last time."

The dad stuffed his hands in his pockets, but Eric's gaze stayed locked on Lou. His intense scowl made goose bumps form on her arms despite the warm sun blanketing them as they waited outside, but Lou knew she had to take advantage of any opening, and him looking at her was an opening. She launched into the question she'd practiced.

"How about that Vicki Younger business, huh?" Lou shook her head and watched the two men.

The other dad nodded, scratching at his chin. "Pretty awful, though it seems like it was inevitable. I wonder why she came back to town in the first place. I would've stayed far away with all that money."

"Right?" Lou widened her eyes. "I thought about that possibility. What if she really didn't run away with everyone's money, and whoever killed her just didn't give her the chance to explain. What about you?" Lou asked Eric. "Why do you think she came back?"

"I have no idea," he said in a tone that had a very *it's none of my business* feel to it.

"But didn't you invest in Vicki's business?" Lou asked, taking a step toward him. "I would think *you'd* be more interested than most in what she was doing back in town." Her hands shook with the adrenaline and nerves of asking such a direct question, so she clasped them behind her back.

Eric's face reddened with anger, and he spat out his response. "Where'd you hear that?"

CHAPTER 9

T he other dad, who stood next to Eric Reynolds, stiffened, glancing around like he wished he could be anywhere else. Lou could relate. Her feet itched to take her away from the angry man.

But the truth wouldn't only help Silas. It would get Noah's family out of hot water with the quilt convention sponsors. She had to know.

"I read on the *BSB* that you were one of the first investors," she admitted, hating how gossipy that made her sound.

Instead of growing angrier, Eric's tight face relaxed. He shook his head. "I backed out at the last minute and didn't invest. I couldn't take that risk with my kids' futures. And it's a good thing I didn't."

The other dad nodded in agreement. He started going on about someone he knew who'd invested, but Lou tuned out the information. She couldn't seem to hear through the blood pounding in her ears in her embarrassment. That's what she got for trusting a gossip blog online.

A bell rang from inside the building, and kids began flooding out. Lou wished she could get out of there, could run away.

Wait. She wasn't waiting for a child like they were. She *could* run. Calling out a quick goodbye, Lou spun away, jogging in the opposite direction. But there were children and parents everywhere. She tried to move out of the way of an excited group of kids and ended up running into the back of a bus. She rubbed at her shoulder and snuck around the bus, taking off at a jog as she rounded the bumper.

Instead, she ran headlong into another person. This one was definitely not a child.

Noah's strong hands gripped her arms, steadying her. "Hey, where are you going in such a hurry?"

Lou simultaneously wanted to melt into him and hide her face in embarrassment. She groaned, glancing over her shoulder to make sure Eric hadn't tried to follow her. "Running away from my bad decisions." She looked up into Noah's dark eyes. He frowned, nonverbally asking for more information. "I just made a fool of myself and unnecessarily embarrassed someone else."

To her surprise, Noah chuckled. His cheeks flushed as he caught her appalled expression. "I'm sorry. I don't mean to laugh. I just can't picture you making a fool of yourself, ever." He guided her away from the throng of families picking up children, buses honking, and teachers waving.

Because the parking lot was crazy, he moved them toward the elementary school building. Noah didn't stop until they'd snuck around the side of the building, and they stood in a small reading garden. It was actually quite peaceful despite the cacophony of noise and movement taking place around the corner.

"Okay, what happened?" he asked, placing a gentle hand on her shoulder.

She leaned her weight into the side of the building and let her temple rest against the brick. "Well, you remember how I was asking about Er—" Stopping herself midword, Lou stood up straight. "Wait, isn't Marigold leaving with Cassidy right after school's out? Do you need to go? I don't want to stop you from getting to say goodbye before she leaves for three weeks." She scooped the air in front of her, beckoning him to walk back toward the last day of school chaos happening behind her.

Reaching out, Noah grabbed on to her hand. "Hey," he whispered.

She froze, her lungs tight at the level of contact. He'd touched her on the hand before, but it was the way he held it now that felt different.

"Cassidy and Marigold are already gone. They pulled away just before I saw you," he explained.

Lou's expression tightened. "Oh, gosh. How are you doing? Are you okay?" Though stoic, she knew this was going to be the longest he'd go without seeing his daughter.

Noah's grip tightened for a moment as he squeezed her hand. His eyes danced with laughter. "Louisa Henry, you're in near crisis, from what I can see, and you're checking on me?"

She placed her free hand on her hip, not missing that he still held on to her other one. "Yes, this is a big deal."

Dipping his head, he said, "I'm okay." His voice cracked

a little around that last word. "Mostly I'm excited for her. I am going to miss her, though. It already feels like a Marigold-sized chunk is missing from my soul."

"I can't even imagine." Lou swallowed to get past the tightness in her throat.

"Now tell me, what's going on with you?" Noah gave her the kind of intense focus that made her feel like he'd do anything to help her.

Puffing out her cheeks, Lou let a breath release slowly. "I just made a fool of myself in front of Eric. I didn't accuse him of murder, thank goodness, but I should've done more research than just checking a gossip blog before talking to him about his 'investment.'" She used finger quotes around the last word.

"What does that mean?" Noah's brow wrinkled.

"He didn't actually invest. He backed out, realizing he couldn't possibly put his family in that situation," Lou explained. "And I'm going to verify that, of course, because he could be lying to keep people off his scent, but I mostly feel silly that I didn't check before I talked to him. It was reckless and a representation of why I should probably leave this case to Roy." She pressed her lips together, self-conscious that she'd just blurted out a lot of emotions.

Noah frowned. "I get your frustration with the situation, but do you really think you're the only one to talk to Eric about that investment? If it was on the *BSB* blog, I can guarantee you he's heard from at least a dozen people in the past twenty-four hours." Noah's eyebrow arched. "In fact, the frustration you experienced from him likely had a lot more to do with how many people have come up to him today instead of you not doing your research."

Lou exhaled a little of the tension she was holding on to. "Oh, that makes sense, actually." Now that she thought about it, Eric had already seemed slightly bothered when she'd approached.

But now that Lou's worries weren't solely focused on how she'd made Eric feel, or how he'd scolded her, she found something new to fret about. A few somethings, actually. One being how close she was standing next to Noah. The second was how secluded everything felt in the reading garden. And the third being that he was still holding her hand.

Suddenly, Lou couldn't feel her fingers or her legs. She stepped back. "You know who would've really liked this reading garden? Ben," she said, her hand sliding out of his. "I'm sorry, I have to go."

Noah's disappointed face blurred along with the rest of her vision as she spun around, breaking into a run. Lou was normally a very calm runner, counting her breaths to make sure she was conserving her energy as she moved. Compared to other runners, Ben especially, she'd never felt particularly fast. Apparently, when she was running from her feelings—quite literally—Lou was incredibly fast. Her breath came in gasps and whooshes, uncontrolled. She cut her normal run time from the elementary school to the bookshop in half.

Chest heaving, she locked the bookshop door behind her and rushed upstairs. Not sure what was going on, the cats, whom she'd left in the bookshop since Catticus was still relegated to the apartment upstairs to rest, raced around her feet, following her up the back staircase. Lou collapsed onto the couch. Tears sprang into her eyes, and her head sank forward, supported by her hands.

A few minutes later, when she was done crying, she pulled out her phone and called Willow. Though her tears had dried up, Lou's fingers still shook as she waited for Willow to pick up the call. The moment her friend answered the phone, however, Lou remembered she wasn't down the road at her house or even up the street at her new nursery. She was hours away in Stoneybrook, having a relaxing vacation with her significant other—in theory, when her best friend wasn't bugging her with problems.

"Hey." Willow's tone was chipper, but there was a definite question hidden within the greeting.

Lou sniffed. "I'm so sorry to bother you. I totally forgot that you were gone until you picked up. It can wait." She tried to make herself sound okay, but Willow could read her like a large-print book.

"Absolutely not." Willow's tone flattened out, turning practically steely. "You're the one person who can call me whenever you need to. You obviously need to talk. What happened?"

Swallowing to give herself a moment to catch her breath from the sobbing, Lou sighed. "I'm not on speakerphone, am I?" she asked in a quiet voice first, smiling a little.

Willow laughed. "No, you're good. Easton's actually at the barn feeding OC and Steve dinner, so it's just the two of us. Spill."

"I just ran after I embarrassed myself in front of Eric Reynolds and then ran away from Noah," Lou blurted out the confession, knowing if she gave herself the chance, she might rethink spilling the truth about the discomfiting afternoon she'd had.

"Okay, I want to know about the Noah thing, but tell me about Eric first," Willow said. Any hint of laughter had disappeared, and she was fully entrenched in Lou's story, needing to know more about her predicament.

Lou explained about her faux pas assuming the information on the *BSB* site to be true.

Willow clicked her tongue. "Ugh. Eric is a jerk, though. He and James used to hang out all the time, and when we got engaged, he told James he was making a big mistake. I wouldn't dwell on that guy." Lou could picture her waving her hand and swiping that worry from the air. "Okay, now tell me about Noah. You ran away from him? Why?"

"He was consoling me after I embarrassed myself in front of Eric. He was holding my hand and looking at me, and"—she swallowed—"I really wanted to kiss him."

Lou could practically feel the energy buzzing off Willow from the other end of the call. To her credit, Willow remained calm as she asked, "Did you?"

"No," Lou responded flatly. "I blurted something about how Ben would've liked the elementary school reading garden and ran away." She pinched the bridge of her nose, frustrated all over again with how she'd handled the situation.

"Oh, Lou-Lou." Willow's voice dropped into a sympathetic register that made Lou feel like a sick kitten, the most pitiful creature around. "I'm so sorry."

"You should tell that to Noah," Lou said. "The poor guy. He was merely being sweet and supportive, and how do I repay him? Blurting random things about my late husband and running away."

A small chuckle escaped from Willow. "Sorry. It's just a funny mental picture."

Lou had to smile. It felt good to do something other than frowning. "I'm sure it was hilarious," she said sarcastically.

"Noah knows you, Lou. I'm sure the only emotion he's experiencing at the moment is worry for you," Willow assured her. "He knows you're going to need time. Why do you think it's been over a year since you moved to town, and he still hasn't made a move, despite the fact that you two are literally perfect for one another? He's gone through a divorce, so he knows what it's like to have his heart broken, and that's on a tenth of the scale of what you went through."

Willow's words, and her familiar voice, calmed Lou.

"Right. I guess I have been asking the universe for a sign about whether I'm ready for love again." Lou sat back on the couch, letting the soft fabric cradle her. "And you can't get much clearer than this. I'm obviously not ready yet since I blurted the name of my dead husband and ran."

Instead of chuckling at Lou's self-deprecating comment, as Lou expected her to, Willow was silent for a beat.

"What?" Lou asked.

"Or maybe it's not a sign from the universe," Willow said carefully. "Maybe it's just you using Ben as an excuse not to get close with someone else because, subconsciously, you're worried about losing another person you love and getting your heart broken again."

Lou swallowed and gulped back the sting of reality Willow's words made her experience.

"Noah needs someone stable, someone who can be there for Marigold." Lou hated that she felt a whiny quality to her words.

"How do you know he needs that? Have you asked him?" Willow was using her firm voice, the one that told OC he was not to mess around with her. And if it worked on the thousand-pound animal, it definitely did with Lou. "Also, how are you not stable for Marigold? You're literally the person who watches her the third most, other than Cass and Noah. She used to hang out at the quilt shop after school, and now I see her at the bookshop more than anywhere else."

Willow had a point. She knew she'd been a steady part of the girl's life and didn't have any plans to change that.

"Let's say all of that is moot, and he wants to try something," Lou said. "What if things don't work out, and I lose the very important friendship I've grown to have with him? What if I lose Marigold?"

Willow clicked her tongue. "Okay, I'll humor you there. If that happened, you *know* how it would go."

"I do?" Lou frowned.

"Look at him and Cassidy. They were married for a decade. They have a daughter together. Cassidy left him for another man, and they're still friends," Willow said. "I mean, you can't get a better guarantee than that, Lou. In fact, I would argue that he's the very best person for you to try moving on with because you know that he's so lovely that you're guaranteed not to lose out on the friendship you have. Neither of you has a petty bone in your body. If things between you didn't work out, I think you'd just go back to being friends. You might even be better friends because there wouldn't be all the tension between you that there is right now."

"You noticed that?" Lou cringed.

"I'm sure even Sapphire has noticed," Willow answered. Then, in a softer tone, Willow added, "Everyone gets it, Lou. You went through something so difficult, most of us can't even fathom it. No one is telling you that you should rush into anything. If you needed to take five years, ten, even twenty, that would be understandable. Heck, if you decided you'd never love again, we would all understand. It just doesn't seem like that's what you want." Willow paused. "Because when I see you look at Noah, it's the same way you used to look at Ben, like he was made of light." Willow's voice tightened as she worked through that last sentence.

Lou's whole body tingled and a chill radiated through her. The moment Willow said it, she knew it was true. Hadn't Olivia, Lou's dear friend, said the same thing when she'd visited over Christmas? Lou's parents had noticed it as well, telling her it was okay to move on when she was ready. Everyone loved Noah. And it wasn't just him. It was how Lou acted around him, how she looked at him. They could tell she had feelings even before she was able to admit that to herself.

"Look," Willow said, knowing Lou needed something more or she would lose herself in her thoughts. "Remember what you told me during Ben's funeral?"

Tears gathered in Lou's eyes again as she remembered that difficult day. "That loving him was something I never wanted to regret." Her voice cracked as she recited the words.

"And if you let the fear of losing someone you love prevent you from falling in love again, isn't that the same thing?" Willow asked.

"Okay. I get it." Lou smiled. "You're very smart. Thank you for the counseling. You should really talk to Forrest about what you could charge me for these support sessions."

"Lou, I'd never charge you," she joked. "You couldn't afford me."

They laughed.

"But seriously. Thank you," Lou said.

"Anytime. Do you feel better? Honest three," Willow said, asking for the first three emotions Lou was feeling in that moment. It was how they'd checked in with each other over the decades, especially when living thousands of miles apart.

"Still overwhelmed, but also clear and a little hopeful." Lou took a deep breath for the first time since she'd run away from Noah. "All thanks to you. Well, I hope you have a good rest of your trip."

"We're going back to the cute brewery again tonight," Willow told her. "Not only was it fantastic, but it's only one of, like, three restaurants around here unless we want to drive up to some city north of here, but everyone in town talks about it like it's worse than Brine, so we're going to stick with what we know." Willow's voice was bright with excitement.

They said their goodbyes, and Lou hopped in the shower, ready to wash the sweat and the memory of the terrible day off her skin. Once she'd changed and was settled on the couch with a book, she realized Willow had solved more than one of her problems.

Not only did she now know she needed to come clean with Noah about her feelings, but she also knew where to go next with the case. Willow's earlier mention of Eric being friends with James had sparked a thought in Lou, one she was going to follow up on. It was too late tonight, but tomorrow, she needed to make a trip to the bank.

CHAPTER 10

As much as the call with Willow had convinced Lou she was ready to talk to Noah about her feelings, she knew she needed to go into that conversation with a clear mind after running away from him at the elementary school. She couldn't do that with worries about Silas being wrongfully accused of murder or the quilting convention losing its sponsors. Once this case was solved, she would be able to focus on Noah.

Lou threw herself into the Vicki Younger case. She had a new lead, after all. Willow's offhand mention of her ex-fiancé yesterday had reminded Lou that, as the manager of the local bank, James might have information about the investors in Vicki's fake business, credible information. She was done with learning things from a gossip site on the internet.

She'd also decided to close early that day if it was as slow as yesterday, which it turned out to be. Lou closed before lunch, hoping things would pick up again once people were done with their initial summer vacations.

After checking on Catticus to make sure he was doing well in her bedroom, she went back to the bank for the second time in as many days. Even though she planned to go inside this time, Lou did take a moment to walk around the building once, thinking about what Silas had told her about the odd things he'd seen Vicki doing before she'd been killed.

"Listening to bricks, kicking at them, clawing at the dirt, and talking to the plants." Lou recited the odd behaviors as she analyzed the bank's exterior and the flower beds that ran around most of the perimeter, except for the entrance and an emergency exit at the back of the building.

But Lou couldn't see anything out of place. None of the bricks were missing, the plants all looked healthy and well watered, and save for a bunch of pine cones and leaves that had blown over from the forest behind the bank, the beds were covered in neatly raked soil.

Feeling like that was a dead end, Lou entered the bank, hoping for something more productive. The interior of the building was nice but dated, like they'd done a remodel about ten years ago. Even though the furniture was still holding up well, they'd gone for a trendy design, and everything was now out of style. One teller stood behind a long counter where bank customers could make deposits or withdrawals. Talking to the teller was James.

James Tippery had seemed like the perfect guy for Willow when they'd met over a decade earlier. A Button native, he'd helped Willow, who'd just moved to town to fill a high school horticulture teaching position, stitch herself in the fabric of the sewing-themed town. She'd been unsure about the place, telling Lou she wasn't sure how long she'd stay, that it might be too small for her.

Then, during a fundraiser at the high school, Willow had met James, the manager of the local bank. He'd been handsome, charming, seemingly the whole package. They moved in together, bought a house together with space for OC, and had been engaged for two years when Willow had caught him cheating with Tiffany Wentz, the very teller he was now talking to, the woman he was engaged to marry.

Even in such a small town, Willow didn't run into James or Tiffany too often, which was good. They'd bought a house in the town of Silver Lake, a bigger town to the south of Button in Lakeside County.

Lou set her jaw and strode over to where James was openly canoodling with his fiancée. Apparently, now that he didn't have to hide their relationship anymore, he was throwing all professionalism out the window. She cleared her throat, hoping one of them might look up and help her since she couldn't see anyone else working.

James lazily glanced over, flinching slightly as he noticed it was Lou standing in front of him. "Louisa, hey." He stepped back, putting some space between him and Tiffany.

"Can I talk to you?" she asked, keeping her tone serious.

Blinking, he said, "Sure."

Motioning to his office behind the row of teller windows, with a nervous flourish of his hands, James left his bride-to-be. He settled into a leather chair behind his large desk and wrung his hands in his lap. Was it just Lou, or did he seem incredibly nervous?

"Wh-what's this about?" he asked.

Hesitation filled Lou. What she was about to ask was against the rules, possibly even breaking a law. James might've taken the promise of fidelity lightly with Willow during their engagement, but she had a feeling he was serious about his job and the responsibilities attached.

"I'm sure you heard about Vicki Younger," Lou started.

James inclined his head. "And Silas." The scowl that accompanied his statement made Lou sure he didn't believe the older man had killed Vicki either. "Are you looking into it?"

It was no secret around town that Lou—and sometimes Willow, by extension—found it hard to keep their noses out of the local cases.

Lou nodded. "I'm trying to, but I just had a terrible run in with Eric Reynolds because I assumed he'd invested, only to find out he didn't, and I wondered if there was any way you had a list of the people who actually invested in Vicki's scheme."

James narrowed his eyes for a moment as he watched Lou. "Even if I did, you know I wouldn't be able to show you that. It's confidential bank information."

"Even if you did?" Lou asked, focusing on what she could glean from his statement. "I thought Vicki had an account here." Lou explicitly remembered Vicki telling people that her business account was housed at the bank in Button, and that was where they could go make investments into her company. It had been one reason residents had felt so comfortable to invest and told their friends to do the same.

"Yes, but we don't have a record of who invested unless they wrote Vicki a check or made a wire transfer. A lot of the locals paid cash." James frowned and scratched at the side of his nose.

The motion told Lou he was keeping something from her. She'd never gotten to know him too well in person, her visits to Willow being brief throughout their years apart, but she'd heard enough about the man through her best friend—so much so that she almost felt like she knew every one of his mannerisms. A nose scratch had usually meant he was holding back information.

Just as Lou was about to call out the man in front of her for lying, his eyes darted up to the open doorway to his office. Lou glanced over her shoulder to see Tiffany Wentz at the threshold. And even though he'd only left the woman moments earlier, and she'd all but had cartoon hearts in her eyes at the time, she seemed incredibly upset now. Her small shoulders hunched with anger, and she stormed over to the desk.

"Babe, I'm in a meeting," James said. His gaze flitted between Tiffany and Lou.

"I just got off the phone with the wedding planner, James." Tiffany's voice trembled with frustration. "You told me you were going to call her yesterday to set a date." She ran a finger under her eye as if she was expecting to find a tear there. "This is the third time I've had to ask. She needs to know what day you want, and you said you'd decide."

Tiffany's statement pinged something in Lou's memory, and what James said next solidified it.

"I know, I'm just having a hard time deciding," he complained to Tiffany.

Lou was transported back to a phone call she'd had with Willow after she'd found James and Tiffany together in his office. Willow had broken into sobs, telling Lou that she'd called off their engagement and asked him to move out.

Willow had said, "I should've known he didn't want to marry me. The man wouldn't even let me set a date for the wedding."

Lou tuned back into the conversation happening with Tiffany and James in front of her as Tiffany leaned down to kiss him and turned to leave.

"I'll send you the wedding planner's number again, just in case you lost it," Tiffany said, just before slipping out the office door.

Lou studied James. His shoulders slumped. He swallowed and pulled in a deep breath before looking back at her.

"Sorry, where were we?" He blinked as if coming out of hypnosis.

"James," Lou whispered.

His eyes reluctantly met hers.

"My brain really likes patterns, so I might be seeing something where there isn't anything," she prefaced. "But you already let one amazing woman go because of your fear of commitment. Do you really want to lose another?" Lou kept her voice low.

She was being modest to suggest that she might be searching for a pattern where there was none. It was by the book the same as it had been with Willow. James and Tiffany had bought a house together and had been engaged for over a year already, with no end in sight, just like Willow and James had been when they'd called everything off.

James exhaled a shaky breath. He raked his fingers through his dark hair.

Lou tensed, unsure if he would snap at her for commenting on his personal life and relationships.

But then James squeezed his eyes shut and said, "You're right." He shook his head and opened his eyes. "I don't want to lose her. I can't. I'll regret it forever if I do."

The way he said that last statement didn't feel like a slight against Willow. No, it wasn't a *Tiffany is so much better than Willow, and I can't lose her even though I could lose Willow* statement. It was definitely an *I can't do this again because I know how much I regretted it the last time* kind of sentiment.

James smiled. Beamed, actually. "I need to go call that wedding planner right now." He stood. Glancing at Lou as if he remembered she was still there, he said, "Thank you." Craning his neck to see into the bank through the open office door, James added, "While I *don't* have a list of the people who invested in Vicki's company, I *do* have the list of bank customers who are always on the lookout for investment opportunities. When Vicki came to me asking for a loan for her start-up, I told her we couldn't fund anything, but I would let the customers on my list know they should get in contact with her for a sales pitch. I know she at least met with a few of them."

Lou was surprised at the sudden flood of information James was sharing.

A sly smile crossed his lips as he pulled out a thin folder from one of his drawer files. "I need to go make that phone call. I'm guessing it'll take me about five minutes." James winked. "I'm going to leave this folder containing the names of the customers we have, who have asked to be notified of investment opportunities, right here while I'm gone," he said, emphasizing each of those last words with a constant widening of his eyes.

"Okay. I'll head out, too, just behind you," Lou said, her heartbeat quickening.

He was going to do her a favor, something he probably shouldn't. She would need to be quick. James rushed out of the office, leaving the door open just a crack.

Standing, Lou rounded his desk and flipped open the folder with one hand while she dug her phone out of her purse with the other. It wasn't a long list. There were only five names on a crisp piece of paper, their phone numbers following each name. And while Lou snapped a quick picture of the page, her gaze caught on one name she recognized.

Francis Knight.

She'd met the man during the last case she worked and had grown quite fond of the eccentric multimillionaire. The fact that his name was on this list didn't look good, however.

It looked like Lou was going to have to make a trip to Brine.

CHAPTER 11

F rancis Knight's mansion was no less impressive the second time.

Lou was obviously not alone in that opinion because as they approached, George said, "Holy money, Batman." She let out a low whistle. "I think my memory downplayed this place, because it's even bigger than I remembered."

While Lou didn't want to believe Francis could've killed Vicki, she still hadn't wanted to show up to his mansion alone to ask questions about his possible investment in the fake company. She'd been wrong about people before. And with Willow out of town, that left George and Brynn, their friend from Brine as backup.

Brynn knew the eccentric billionaire better than any of them since she and her dad were Mr. Knight's landscapers. When Lou had approached Brynn about coming with her to talk to him, she'd been instantly interested.

Lou had driven, unlike their first visit when they'd all piled into Brynn's Pine Landscaping truck, so there was a hint of wariness behind the butler's voice as it came through the speaker on the other side of the large gate, and he asked how he could help them.

"Hi, Stuart," Lou said cheerily. "My name is Louisa Henry. I visited a couple of months ago with Brynn Pine."

"Hey, Stu," Brynn called from the back seat.

"We have a few questions for Mr. Knight, if he's available," Lou said.

Silence stretched through the speaker.

"It's about another murder mystery," Lou added, remembering how much Francis had enjoyed helping them with their last case.

Something buzzed, and the gates slowly swung open.

"Come in," Stuart said.

George clapped her hands excitedly as if they were driving into a theme park instead of up to someone's home. But with the tropical plants crowding the yard, and the themed rooms inside the enormous estate, it *was* kind of a theme park.

She parked in the circular driveway, just as Brynn had last time they came. The large double doors opened. Francis stood in the entryway instead of Stuart. The bored butler waited a few yards behind. It was as if they were playing opposites. For as bored as Stuart appeared, Francis practically buzzed.

Despite the hot temperatures outside, it was almost too cold inside the mansion, and Francis wore the same velvet smoking jacket he had worn the last time they met.

"Louisa, what a pleasure." He reached for her hand, kissing it. His graying mustache tickled the back of her hand. "Brynn, lovely as always." He bowed to her. Then his gaze landed on George. "And our techie friend, George. Welcome." Francis lightly tapped his long fingers together. "Shall we talk in the dining room? I was just about to sit down to lunch, and you would be very welcome to join me."

Lou had left home in a hurry once the plan to see Francis had come together, and she hadn't even thought about lunch. Her stomach growled at the suggestion.

"Sounds great," Brynn said, matching George's interested expression.

Stuart led them to a room that held a table, which had to be at least twenty feet long. Lou was sure they wouldn't be able to hear each other if they sat at opposite ends, so she was glad when Francis settled at the head of the table and pointed to the seats next to him for them to occupy.

Once they were seated, and each had a freshly squeezed lemonade in hand, Stuart bustled in with a tray featuring gorgeously plated meals.

"Roasted chicken with seasonal vegetables and risotto," Francis explained as Stuart placed a plate in front of each of them.

"Thank you, this looks amazing," Lou said, barely able to get the words out before she tried her first bite. The food was delicious.

They must've all been hungry because the table was silent as they ate their meals, no one wanting to stop long enough to start a conversation. But once Lou had eaten her fill, she said, "Well, I'm sure you've heard about the woman who was found strangled in Button on Wednesday."

Francis raised a single finger, swallowing the final bite

he'd been chewing. "I did. So sad." Francis placed his napkin and fork on his dish.

"Did she talk to you about investing?" Lou asked.

Francis nodded. "I can usually see a scam from a mile away, but she was good. In the end, I didn't invest because of what she said about your fine town."

Lou and George shared a confused glance.

"Our town?" George blurted, pushing her plate away to show she was also done eating.

Francis looked solemn as he said, "She went on a diatribe about how she'd bought a house there without doing her research in the area and found it stuffy and fake. She liked Brine much better and spent most of her time here anyway." He smiled at Brynn as if they should be proud of that compliment.

Lou barked out a laugh. "That's the same thing she said about you guys."

"She played us against each other." George scratched at her temple.

"So she never had a house in either town. She must've just been sleeping in her car the whole time," Lou guessed, talking more to herself than anyone else at the table. That would explain why Silas had found blankets and a pillow in her car when he'd searched it. "It's kind of brilliant, if you think about it."

Talking badly about the neighboring town and playing on the deep-seated rivalry had helped Vicki quickly gain the trust of both towns. Brine and Button may be neighbors, but they couldn't be more different. And because of that, they were constantly at odds.

Francis clicked his tongue. "And I'd just met you,

George, and Willow. I couldn't dare invest with someone who spoke so poorly of my newfound friends. Not to mention Ribs. He's had nothing but wonderful things to say about your town."

Ribs Randall was an old army pal of Francis's. And while they'd ended up in very different circumstances, once immersed in civilian life, they remained close. Ribs said they had dinner each month as long as Francis wasn't out of the country for one reason or another.

Pushing through the incredulity brought up because of the new information they had about Vicki's scam, Lou realized that answered the question they'd come there to answer.

"So you didn't invest," she said, pulling out the most important detail from what he'd said.

Francis shook his head. "Thank goodness."

George exhaled in frustration. Her cheeks turned pink as she said, "Sorry, I'm not mad that you didn't lose money. I just feel like that leaves us at a dead end."

While Lou shared in George's feelings of hopelessness for a moment, she reminded herself that things weren't completely lost. She still had four other names on the list from the bank. Francis had merely been their first stop.

Brynn gripped the arms of her chair and was about to stand when Francis held up a bony hand.

"I may not have invested, but I know someone who did," Francis crooned.

The three women leaned forward in anticipation.

"Sebastian Andrade invested in Vicki Younger's company." Francis lifted his chin.

"Sebastian Andrade?" Lou hadn't heard of him. That

wasn't saying much, as she hadn't heard of Francis until a few months ago either. "Is he in Brine too?"

"Button, technically." Francis sighed as Stuart bustled in to grab their dishes. "He lives on the hill just inside the town limits."

Lou blinked. She knew there was a hill behind the downtown area, but she'd never seen a house on it.

George placed her hands on the table, palms down. "He's the man on the hill?"

Brynn and Lou looked from Francis to George, hoping for clarification.

"Man on the hill." Brynn snorted. "Sounds like some weird myth."

George shrugged. "It kind of is. That hill behind Button is prime real estate. From that perspective, you get a direct view of the Cascade Range and can see out over the valley, not to mention the river snaking through it. But no one can build there because someone's always owned the whole thing, all the land."

"Sebastian's great-grandfather bought those fifty acres, and they built one house on the hill," Francis explained. "Exactly one."

George took over the story. "He lives up there alone. No one's ever seen him. No one's allowed on the property. We've never even been able to see a house."

Francis chuckled. "That's on purpose, I assure you."

"So…?" George asked. "What's he like?"

"He's a man who lives on a hill," Francis said with a shrug, as if that were more than enough description.

Lou tapped her toes in excitement. "And you said he invested in Vicki's business? How do you know?"

Francis pursed his lips. "He told me."

"Did he invest the ten grand everyone else did, or did he lose even more?" Brynn asked, touching on a good point. Ten grand was a lot to normal people, but it wouldn't be enough to make a rich person like Francis or Sebastian mad enough to kill.

"Oh, much more," Francis answered.

"Like, how much?" Brynn asked.

The corners of Francis's eyes crinkled into a smile. He regarded Brynn as if she were a sweet child who'd just asked why the sky was blue. "Money is relative," he said slowly, obviously stepping around their feelings.

Brynn gulped.

"Could it buy a car, house, or country?" Lou asked, making up a quick scale to help them move forward.

It wasn't until Francis squinted in thought that she realized their definition of cars and houses was also vastly different. Both Lou and George's homes could've fit inside the main entryway to Francis's mansion. And even though Brynn's farmhouse was large, she shared the space with her father.

"A car. Definitely." Francis punctuated his statement with a nod, showing he was sure.

"That's still a lot," George whispered in awe.

"Enough to kill over?" Lou asked, knowing the clarification was important.

Francis let out a "psh" sound that told Lou it wasn't. "Investments often do not pan out as we hope."

"So you don't think we should talk to him?" George asked, confusion marring her features.

Francis blinked. "No, you definitely should. Let's just

say that Sebastian likes to know everything about a company when he invests. He would have a list of investors that might help you narrow down who would've wanted her dead."

Excitement bubbled in Lou. That was just what she'd been hoping for when she'd gone to talk to James. But warning bells sounded in her mind. "If he does so much research on the companies he invests in, how didn't he catch that Vicki's was fake, that she planned to steal the money and run?"

"That's a good question," Francis said. "One you'll have to ask him. I don't know."

"Will he even talk with us?" George asked, clinging to the fairy-tale feeling of the mysterious and reclusive man on the hill.

"He will if I ask him," Francis said with a devilish grin.

Unease worked through Lou's stomach. She didn't want to put them in danger by waltzing into a killer's home. "Will you come with us?" Lou asked. She wasn't sure what it was about the eccentric man, but as much as he surprised her with his interesting taste and childlike curiosity, she trusted him.

Beaming, Francis said, "I thought you'd never ask."

CHAPTER 12

Francis placed a very loud call to Sebastian, boldly inviting himself and his guests over to talk about Vicki Younger and her fake company. Lou couldn't hear the other side of the conversation, but either Sebastian was excited to have them, or Francis was intimidating to both rich and regular people alike.

"He can see us right now, if you can spare the time," Francis said to the group after he finished his phone call.

Lou checked with Brynn and George before saying, "Sure."

As much as Lou would've loved to ride in one of Francis's fancy cars, driven around by Stuart like they were royalty, she didn't want to leave her car behind if they were driving to Button anyway.

Brynn rode with them, saying she'd catch a ride with Francis on the way back to Brine.

"I can't believe I'm going to meet the man on the hill." George let out a little squeal of excitement. "No one's going to believe me."

"What do you think he's going to look like?" Brynn asked George, the keeper of the myths and legends about the man on the hill.

George didn't even need to think. "Old. Maybe even older than Francis."

Lou stifled a chuckle. The two young women in their twenties talked about Lou and Willow as if they were ancient, and they weren't even forty yet. Francis, probably in his sixties, was archaic to them.

It was a good thing Lou was following Stuart as they approached the hill. No matter how welcome Francis assured them they would be, she would've turned around at the gates and the signage posted around the sizable hill.

She felt as though they were waiting to drive into Jurassic Park as the large wooden gates swung open and Francis's car crept through the opening in front of them. The road that meandered up the hill was pristinely paved, instead of being a dirt or pebble-covered rural road like Lou was used to seeing on private drives.

Suddenly, they emerged from the trees and saw a modern structure. The house was all sharp lines and large windows. Following Stuart around the round driveway, Lou parked as George and Brynn gasped in awe of the house.

Stuart slipped out of the sleek, black car first, striding around to the other side to let out Francis. Lou and the girls disembarked from her car, staring and blinking as they slammed their doors shut.

The probably hand-carved wooden front door opened, and out stepped a man around Lou's age. Assuming things were the same as at Francis's home, Lou figured he must be

Sebastian's butler. Still, his appearance took Lou by surprise.

While Stuart was dressed in the standard butler uniform one might've seen back in the days of British lords and ladies owning large estates, Sebastian's butler was dressed in what Lou had grown up thinking of as the Pacific Northwest dress code: jeans or khakis paired with some kind of outdoor fleece or T-shirt. Given that it was summer, his khaki shorts and black T-shirt fit the bill. But still seemed entirely too casual for someone's butler.

"Frannie," the man said, holding out a hand to shake Francis's as he stepped forward.

"Sebastian." Francis took his hand and shook, holding on a little too long, as if they were having a quick arm wrestle.

Lou's mouth parted in surprise. That was Sebastian, not a butler. But he was so young, handsome, and answering his own door. After hanging out with Francis, she'd assumed all ridiculously rich people would act the same. Then she reminded herself that in New York City, there had been just as many wealthy people who used their money to buy up warehouses in Brooklyn to turn into rustic homes as there were those who bought into the fancy penthouse life with a doorman and waitstaff.

Sebastian's age wasn't just a surprise to Lou either. George and Brynn stared as they took in the suave-looking man.

Breaking away from the handshake, Sebastian turned his thousand-watt—or make that million-watt—smile toward them. "The famous George of George's Technology Emporium," he said, shaking George's hand first and then

Brynn's. Finally, he turned to Lou. "And you must be Louisa." He took her hand firmly and shook it as if they were equals in a business deal. "I've heard of the great things you're doing at your bookstore," he said with a small bow of his head.

"You have?" she asked, caught off guard before she remembered what Francis said about him doing his research into his investments. It would make sense that he also kept tabs on the town he looked out on every day.

"I have a soft spot for cats, as you'll see inside." Sebastian smiled, showing off beautiful teeth that spoke of either amazing genes or expensive dental work.

He swept his hand toward the great door, jogging ahead to hold it open for them. Feeling like Dorothy stepping inside the Emerald City, Lou reminded herself to keep her mouth closed as she wandered into the beautiful foyer.

Whereas Francis's mansion was ornate, gold, and flashy, Sebastian's was focused on nature. The floors were made of enormous slabs of stone. The occasional vein of a rusty orange color or a splash of green which ran through the stone offset the dark gray tones in the slabs. Down a few steps sat a living room that took Lou's breath away. Not only did the room hold the largest single-paned window Lou had ever encountered, but the walls on either side were adorned with … cat trees.

These weren't like the standard kind Lou had in her apartment back home, with pieces of carpet attached to wood. These cat trees could double as art installations. Pieces of beautiful wood created pathways along the walls, moving up to hammocks or small bridges.

Lou might not have believed animals were allowed on

the fancy pieces, except that about a dozen cats dozed in different positions throughout the space.

"See?" Sebastian smirked as he walked up next to her, beaming at the many felines.

"This is amazing." Lou stretched her arms out as she took it all in. "And I thought *I* had a lot of cats. I think you have twice as many as I do."

He shrugged. "Gotta do some good with all of this money."

"Are they all rescues?" Lou asked, as a thin tortoiseshell cat trotted over to greet her.

"They are," Sebastian said, his chest puffing out a bit in pride.

"Aren't you a sweet one," Lou said as she bent to greet the cat, who was now rubbing up against her calves.

Sebastian chuckled. "That's Meatball. I found her in the city about a month ago. She had a meatball clutched in her teeth and just about took my hand off when I tried to grab her." He rubbed at his wrist as if he still remembered the bite. "She's not really a fan of me, unfortunately. I think she had a few less-than-ideal run-ins with men before I found her, and she feels more comfortable with women." He motioned down to where Meatball was now stretched out at Lou's feet, as if to prove his point.

Lou surveyed the room. "How do you know she prefers women?" she asked, noting that there didn't seem to be anyone else in the house.

"She cowers around me and other men but runs right up to any woman who steps foot in the house, as she just did with you. Meatball also loves my cook, Lisa," he answered. "But Lisa has a pretty territorial cat of her own at home and can't take Meatball, as much as she wants to."

"I could take her if you want," Lou blurted out before she even had a moment to consider what she was offering. She sucked in a sharp breath, surprised by her offer. But as she studied the cat at her feet, she realized it wasn't all that wild of an idea.

Sebastian beamed. "That would be amazing. I love having her around, but I can tell she'd be happier where there are some women. Are you sure it wouldn't be an imposition? She's all up to date on her vaccines and vet appointments."

"Not at all." Lou leaned down to pet the cat. "I'm happy to help make her more comfortable."

A sharp elbow landed in Lou's side. She flinched and cut her gaze to the right where George stood, glaring at Lou. Awareness washed over her, along with a pang of guilt. They weren't there for her to make a new best friend and talk about cats. There was a murderer on the loose in their town, and as of that moment, their friend was taking the fall for it.

"We should get to business, shouldn't we?" Sebastian asked, proving he'd caught the interaction.

George and Brynn simultaneously said, "Yes" and plopped into the chairs in the living room that had sweeping views of the Skagit Valley and the Cascade Mountain Range beyond.

Lou settled on the large sectional couch next to them, while Sebastian took a seat in a chair facing them, his back to the amazing view. Francis perched on the far edge of the couch.

"So," Sebastian said, settling his hands in his lap, "you want to know about Vicki and the investment I made."

Lou, George, Brynn, and even Francis nodded emphatically.

Sebastian swallowed, pulling in a deep breath as if it were a long story and he had to prepare. "It's not my proudest moment, but you live and learn, right?"

"Before we get into that, where were you on Wednesday around five o'clock?" George asked.

Sebastian didn't appear flustered at all. Lou knew that meant little since some people were quite good at hiding their true feelings, but when he added, "I was in the air, on my way back from seeing my family on the East Coast," she figured they could trust him.

"You could've hired someone," Brynn added, reminding Lou that she'd, yet again, failed to think of that.

This Sebastian character was catching her completely off guard.

He dipped his chin. "True. But hiring someone to kill her would cost more than I invested in the first place." Sebastian glanced at Francis, and they shared a knowing smirk.

George gulped in discomfort as Lou wondered if that had been a joke. The fact that she couldn't be sure made her squirm uncomfortably in her seat.

Francis cleared his throat. "I was telling Louisa here that you might have a list of the other investors, so she could look into them as possible suspects in Vicki's murder."

Sebastian took a beat to answer. "I do have a list."

It was Lou's turn to notice the details that weren't adding up. George and Brynn shouldn't have to do all the legwork there. She narrowed her eyes at the handsome, charming man. "If you looked into Vicki and the investment, how did you miss it being a pyramid scheme?"

"That's the even more embarrassing part." Sebastian winced. "Normally, I would have my PI look into the company and even follow the creator around to make sure they're legitimate. But Vicki was superb at lying. Sure, it was easy enough to see it was a pyramid scheme, but plenty of those have made people money in the past before they fall apart. I was willing to hear her out. She came to the pitch meeting with a list of other investors already written out for me. Plus, it was such a small amount in the grand scheme of things. I didn't think I needed to employ the same tactics I usually did to check up on a company. It turns out, doing so might've saved a lot of people their savings and Vicki her life. And for that, I'm sorry."

"Can we see the list?" Lou asked.

Sebastian got up from his seat to go to a file cabinet hidden in the wall next to the kitchen. Lou blinked in surprise. He pulled a single paper out of a folder and handed it over to Lou.

At first glance, it was the people she knew about, with the exception of a few names she didn't recognize. They must be the investors from Brine.

"You can keep that. I made a copy when Francis told me you were interested." He sat down again. "But I think you're wrong to focus on the people on that list."

Lou frowned, looking up from the paper. "Why?"

"Even though I didn't do the same amount of research I normally would, I can tell Vicki's 'company' was run well, and the scam was airtight. Not to take away from her skills, because she was obviously a talented con artist, but I suspect Vicki wasn't working alone."

"How?" Lou asked.

"Conning people out of that much money isn't something you're automatically good at," Sebastian explained. "It takes practice, which means she's done this before. We're not her first marks. That also means she probably had a scout." He raised an eyebrow.

"And you think her scout turned against her so he or she could keep all the money they scammed people out of?" George asked with a gasp.

Sebastian wet his lips. "That's exactly what I think happened."

CHAPTER 13

Lou had to admit, Sebastian's theory about a partner being more likely to kill Vicki than one of her investors was compelling. But even the beautiful view out of the panoramic windows overlooking the valley in his hillside mansion didn't make this conversation any more pleasant.

"So we need to figure out if Vicki was working with a partner." Lou tapped her foot as thoughts populated her overwhelmed brain.

"I could have my PI look into it, if you want," he offered.

"Sure." Lou nodded. "Couldn't hurt, right? Maybe have them start in Brine specifically. We can start looking on our end in Button."

"Francis and I can ask around in Brine too," Brynn offered, gesturing to the velvet-clad man perching on the corner of the couch.

"Absolutely," Francis said. "As I've said before, I—"

"*You know people,*" Lou, Brynn, George, and Sebastian all

said in unison, laughing at how in sync their sarcasm had been in the moment.

Francis chuckled. "Ah, you've heard. Good." He didn't seem at all embarrassed.

They spent the next few minutes exchanging phone numbers so Sebastian could get ahold of them if his PI found anything, or vice versa. But if Lou thought that was the ending of their time in the house on the hill, she was sorely mistaken.

"Do you have time to stay for a tour?" Sebastian asked, his eyes lighting up at the prospect of showing his guests around his property.

Francis opened his hands toward the women, as if to remind them that he was completely free that afternoon. Brynn nodded, and so did George when Lou looked in her direction.

"Sure," Lou said with a shrug. "We'd love to see the place."

Sebastian began with a tour of the house, showing off the rest of his cats and the different architectural design decisions he'd made to accommodate them. Next, he took them on a tour of his expansive garage, during which George asked what the two golf carts parked in the corner were for.

Sebastian's eyes sparkled. "Hop in. I'll show you."

He drove George and Lou in one cart, while Stuart operated the second, holding Francis and Brynn. They started out on small pathways branching out from the house. They were pristine and paved, like miniature roadways, made just wide enough for the golf carts.

Lou stared down the hill and saw that similar pathways

crisscrossed all over the hillside under the trees. She grabbed onto the roof as Sebastian took a turn onto a path leading up the hill.

"They make great running or walking paths when I'm not using them to drive on," Sebastian narrated as he drove, noticing Lou admiring them.

"I bet." The thought of running along these quiet, wooded pathways sounded equally peaceful and like a great workout.

Winding up the hill, Sebastian pointed out little things here and there like his favorite gnarly tree or a place where he accidentally tipped one of the golf carts over last fall. But the true reason for the trip became clear once they came to the summit of the hill, where the trees thinned and a rocky outcropping created a vantage point that looked out across the valley, rivaling the view from his fancy living room.

"Wow." For the second time that day, Lou felt like she was reliving parts of the *Jurassic Park* movie, this time plucking the sunglasses from her eyes so she could get a better view of the amazing sights, just like Dr. Grant did when he first saw the dinosaurs in the park.

"Why didn't you build your house up here?" George asked in awe.

Lou shot her a glare as the second golf cart finally caught up with them.

"What?" George complained. "It's an even better view than he's got down there."

Sebastian chuckled. "It's okay. She's not wrong. It *is* the best location on the entire hill, but when your goal is privacy above all else, you make sacrifices."

Saddened by his response, and the fact that he felt the need to hide away from the world, Lou wandered over to a hand-carved bench that sat at the summit. She pulled in a few deep breaths while those in the second golf cart climbed out and marveled at the views.

Beautiful as it was, the late afternoon sun was beating down on them and they returned to the golf carts after a short while. Sebastian didn't return to the garage, however. He drove them all the way down the hill, giving them a full tour of his property.

When he invited them to stay for dinner once they'd finally returned to the garage, Lou got the acute impression that Sebastian was lonely. They all agreed to stay, especially when he explained that his cook had made fresh sushi that afternoon and had left it for him that evening.

Lou waited until she was dipping a piece of sashimi in soy sauce to ask Sebastian, "Why don't you come down to Button more often?"

Having just placed a piece of sushi in his mouth, Sebastian contemplated her question as he chewed. "I think a lot of it has to do with my father, and my grandfather before him. They were both paranoid men, sure everyone was out for their money," Sebastian answered after he'd swallowed.

Brynn's gaze flashed over to Francis, who cleared his throat and became increasingly interested in his plate, telling Lou she had talked to him about having the same tendencies.

Lou popped the sashimi in her mouth, almost closing her eyes at the buttery softness of the fresh fish and how it mixed with the salty soy sauce and vinegary rice. She swallowed. "I've only been living there for a year and a half, but I love it. The people are wonderful, and there's always something in town to get involved in."

At that comment, Sebastian's eyes narrowed slightly.

Realizing her mistake, Lou added, "Not monetarily. No one needs your money. It's about giving your time and helping make Button a better place. I've made some of my best friends by getting involved in town events." She smiled over at George, but the person she was really thinking about was Noah. "It was one of those friends who gave me the idea to use my bookstore as a cat rescue sanctuary in the first place."

Sebastian's eyes remained narrowed as he listened, but it was clear that his thoughts had switched from being suspicious to contemplative. "You know, that's not such a bad idea. Thank you for the suggestion, Lou. Will you let me know the next time there's something happening where I might volunteer my time?"

Lou promised she would, and they chatted about the different festivals and events coming up in each of their respective towns. Lou felt like laughing at the difference between Button and Brine, highlighted simply by the types of events they hosted.

Whereas Button was in the middle of its annual quilting convention, Brine was finishing up a fried-pickle fest, which Brynn described as an ongoing search for the best fried-pickle recipe in the state.

"No, it's a really big deal," Brynn said when they chuckled at her description. "Henry Long's recipe won for three years in a row, but he was taken out by Jeff Marsh this year." She blinked at them, unable to fathom how they couldn't see what a big deal that was.

Even Francis, who also lived in Brine, shrugged in confusion with the Buttonites.

Once they'd had their fill of sushi, Sebastian got Meatball all set to go home with Lou, telling her she could bring the cat back at any time if it wasn't a great fit. He had a spare cat carrier, and he went over all of the cat's likes and dislikes as he got her settled inside. Sebastian promised to be in touch about whatever his PI found, and Lou told him he was welcome at the bookshop anytime.

Cat in hand, Lou and George said goodbye to Francis and Brynn before parting ways. After dropping George off at home, Lou went to the bookstore and got Meatball set up in her office for the night. She and George had agreed to meet at the coffee shop the next morning before she opened the bookshop to figure out what their next step was in finding Vicki's murderer. And after the day she had, Lou fell asleep almost immediately when her head hit the pillow.

The next morning, she fed the cats early and trotted across the street to the Bean and Button, the local coffee shop and one of the best places in town to pick up the latest gossip.

The windows were open, allowing the cool morning breeze to waft through the space. The plastic buttons, with cartoons or funny sayings, covered most of the walls and the front of the counter that separated the customers from the baristas. George stood just inside the shop, waiting for Lou. Sharing a tired greeting, the two stepped up to order.

Ruby, the shop manager, stood behind the counter with

her salt-and-pepper hair pulled up into a messy bun. "Good morning," she said. "What can I get you today?"

Lou and George shared a quick look and a shrug. It was too early to have to decide.

"Surprise us?" George suggested with a laugh.

Ruby's eyes lit up. "Oh, I just got in something new. I've been dying to try it out on some customers." She rubbed her hands together. "It'll be no charge, and I can make you something else if you hate it, but I'd love your input."

"Sure." Lou blinked. She loved the idea of trying new things, often feeling as if she got into ruts with what she liked to eat and drink.

Ruby got to work behind the counter, the steamer screaming as it heated the milk and the sound of a grinder working through the beans. Lou and George settled at the table by the front window, watching as people passed by on the street.

"Okay, so Sebastian mentioned looking into an accomplice, someone who helped Vicki." Lou tapped her fingers on the table as she thought. "When he talked about a scout yesterday, that made me think we might be looking for someone who showed up a month or so before Vicki came to town."

It was then that Lou realized George wasn't listening at all. She was staring out the window, a daydreamy look on her face.

Lou snapped her fingers. "Hey. What's going on?"

George blinked. "Sorry, I think I'm still reeling from yesterday. I can't believe I met the man on the hill, not to mention spent hours touring his whole property. Sebastian is so down to earth too. Well, maybe my experience with

Francis left me with an incorrect assumption about million-aires, but he seemed like such a laid-back guy."

Lou agreed. "The Andrade house was amazing. I'm kind of worried Meatball is going to have too high of standards to live in the bookshop." She chuckled.

"Who would've thought he's almost more of a cat person than you." George shook her head.

Ruby bustled over with a mug in each hand. "Okay, so I want you to take a sip first, and then I'll tell you what it is." Excitement practically pulsed through her veins.

"It's coffee, though, right?" George asked as she examined the light-brown liquid in the mug in front of her after Ruby set it down.

Ruby laughed. "Yes. It's coffee. It should have a nuttiness to it, and you taste some chocolate as well."

Raising an eyebrow, they nodded at each other, and each took a sip.

Lou let the hot liquid settle over her tongue, holding it in her mouth for a moment to savor the flavors before swallowing. Ruby was right. It was delightfully nutty, and there was just a hint of bitter chocolate at the back of her palate.

Her eyes widened. "That's really delicious," Lou told Ruby, going in for another sip.

"It is," George said after she'd swallowed. "What kind of coffee is it?"

"White coffee." Ruby beamed. "It's still coffee beans, but they're roasted at a much lower temperature. I thought it might be fun for people who like less bitterness in their cup. I didn't love it so much with plain milk, but I made it like a mocha, and it really seems to shine."

Lou licked some of the foam from her lip. "It definitely does."

Ruby clapped. "I'm so glad you like it. Thanks for being my test subjects."

They raised their mugs to her as she jogged over to help a new customer. While Ruby got to work on a new order, Lou and George moved on from gushing about their time with Sebastian last night and started thinking about their problem at hand.

"Okay, sorry. I'm ready to do some digging about Vicki's accomplice." George set down her coffee. "But I think you're wrong to discount the possibility that someone local might've helped her."

Lou's stomach clenched in discomfort at the suggestion. But George was right. As awful as it felt to consider, someone from Button could've helped Vicki in her scam. If she'd run away before paying them whatever cut she'd promised, they might've tried to get revenge once she showed up in town again.

"Let's split up. You ask about people who were from out of town," George suggested. "And I'll focus on figuring out which townspeople she spent time with."

Lou nodded. "Good plan." Checking her watch, Lou said, "I have thirty minutes until I have to open the bookshop. Meet back here in twenty?"

They worked the crowded coffee shop for about twenty minutes. Lou had just finished talking to Adam the mailman, who had no helpful information and just wanted to vent about the rise in junk mail, when she noticed George sit down at their same table once more. Making her excuses to Adam, Lou headed in that direction.

"Find anything?" Lou asked as she sat across from her friend.

George leaned close. "There was one name that kept coming up, repeatedly." She paused for effect, eyeing Lou before saying, "James."

"Tippery?" Lou practically gasped out the bank manager's last name.

"Yeah," George said. "People saw Vicki go to the bank a lot, which makes sense since she was using the bank to collect the investments for the company, but they mentioned her hanging out with James, too, like, more than she needed to for banking needs."

Lou's mind was like a runaway train, charging toward an idea. She hadn't thought too hard about how James had been dragging his feet with the wedding preparations, assuming that had been the only symptom showing of his pattern of having cold feet. But he hadn't *just* dragged out decisions when he'd been engaged to Willow. He'd also cheated on her with Tiffany.

What if James had fallen into the same pattern this time around too?

Had he and Vicki been involved? Vicki had been a beautiful woman and was about the same age, if not a little younger. In the wake of her disappearance, people had discussed her charm as a reason why she'd been able to convince so many locals to trust her. A romantic relationship, especially when he was already engaged to someone else, would make James a suspect in Vicki's murder. That, added to how she'd been hanging around the bank the day she died, made it seem like even more of a possibility.

But Lou kept the thought to herself. The idea was just

that—a wondering—not even worth saying aloud to George just yet.

She moved on to sharing her news. "On my front, the only person who had anything to say was Nikki," Lou said, mentioning one of the cashiers at the grocery store. "She noticed a man hanging around town a lot the month before Vicki showed up. She said he was retired, bald, tanned, wearing shorts and flip-flops, and had a huge white beard. She hasn't seen him since, though."

"That could be something," George said. "Why don't we keep asking around and meet again tomorrow morning before you open the bookshop to discuss what we find?"

Lou yawned. "Or, I could close tomorrow, so we have all day."

While the tourist traffic made it too lucrative to close on the weekends, Lou often closed early on Mondays and Tuesdays since they were her slowest sales days. Every once in a while, however, she found she needed a full day off and posted special hours.

"Sounds good," George said.

They finished their white coffees and left.

THE NEXT MORNING, Lou waited at the bookstore for George, but she got a text that told her to meet at the coffee shop instead. Although she didn't understand why since they'd already asked around about Vicki there yesterday, Lou got ready and crossed the street.

The young woman was already sitting at the same table, frowning.

"Hey. What's up?" Lou slid into the seat across from her before going to order.

George set down her phone. "Uh, I don't know." She narrowed her eyes at Lou. "You... There isn't... I—" she cut out, putting an end to the string of unfinished sentences.

Lou had never seen her friend speechless. "Is everything okay?"

George pulled in what looked to be a fortifying breath. "Are you the *BSB*?" she asked, blurting the question out in a whisper as if she'd been worried she'd change her mind if she didn't just rip off the bandage and ask.

Head jerking back in surprise, Lou let out an involuntary snort. "No. What would make you think that?"

Waking up her phone, George spun it around and slid it over to Lou. On the screen was the *BSB* blog, pulled up to the latest post. It had been published last night.

"The man on the hill identified!" was the title along the top. Lou's eyes traveled down to the body of the post.

I have confirmed Sebastian Andrade as the mysterious million-aire who lives on the hill behind the town of Button. He's described as being down to earth and having a love for cats, but is he really a man of the people? How can he be when he owns such a large plot of land and hides himself away from those surrounding him? I'll be doing more research into these questions, so stay tuned for more information, Button.

"You're the only other person around here that knew that. I didn't tell anyone." George's eyes bore into Lou as she read.

Lou shook her head emphatically. "I didn't tell anyone, either, and this isn't me."

They glanced over at Ruby, in unison.

"Do you think it could be?" George whispered.

Lou shrugged. "I wouldn't have thought so, but we had that conversation here. I suppose people could've overheard us from nearby tables."

Even as Lou said it, she didn't know how it could be true. She and George had been quiet, and there hadn't been anyone sitting or standing near them at the time. Trying to think of an alternative, Lou glanced out the window.

Across the street, Noah walked up to the bookstore, causing Lou's breath to catch in her throat at the sight of him. She hadn't seen him since she'd run away from him that day after school had let out. Cupping his hands, he looked in the bookshop window, then glanced at the Closed sign on the door. Lou slowly leaned back so she wouldn't be visible through the front window of the coffee shop, just in case he looked that way.

George flicked a finger toward Lou. "What's going on here? Are you hiding from him?"

Heat flushed over Lou's face, and she swallowed, not sure what to say. "I might be," she croaked out the admission.

Leaning forward, George asked, "Ooh. Why? Did something happen between you and Noah?"

It was odd for Lou to talk to anyone but Willow about these kinds of feelings, but she knew it usually felt better when she got them off her chest.

Lou nodded, then immediately shook her head. "I mean, nothing's happened yet, but I think I want something to, and it's freaking me out. I'm not sure how to go from being friends to more but it seems like lately we're always just a few inches from kissing."

"Lou, that's amazing." George jumped up and down in her seat.

"I just don't know—" But before she could finish that statement, a fancy black car pulled up in front of the shop, causing Lou to freeze.

CHAPTER 14

Noah, who'd pulled out his phone—probably to text Lou—was still standing in front of Whiskers and Words when Sebastian Andrade stepped out of the car. Noah's dark eyes narrowed at the unfamiliar man, and Lou sucked in a breath.

"Is that Sebastian?" George gasped. "Do you think he reads the *BSB* too? What if he thinks we told?"

The possibility that he was upset, and here to confront her from spilling his secret, made Lou feel sick. Added to the way Noah was appraising him, Lou knew she couldn't hide any longer.

"I should go," Lou said, standing and rushing for the door.

George stayed put, but Lou caught her staring out the front window of the coffee shop when she checked back over her shoulder. Noah and Sebastian were eyeing each other warily when Lou approached. Her stomach was in knots as she bounded over to them, waving at Noah first before she turned to the other man.

"Sebastian. Hi." She smiled, hoping it didn't look fake. "What brings you to this part of town?" Her voice was definitely shaking.

"Sebastian?" Noah asked. And even though he stopped there, it was easy enough to fill in the "like, from the *BSB* post about the man on the hill?" subtext of his question.

"The man on the hill, at your service," Sebastian said with a bow.

He'd seen the blog post.

Lou's stomach sank. "Sebastian, I'm so sorry. I promise George and I didn't tell anyone. I don't know how they found out." She waited for Sebastian to berate her for taking only a matter of days to leak a secret he and his family had kept for decades.

"It's okay," Sebastian said instead. "After what you said about getting involved more in the community, I think it's for the best. Now that they know who I am, I don't have any reason to stay away."

Noah watched the man in awe, much like George had when she'd first come face-to-face with the mythical man.

"If you're not mad about the post, what are you doing here?" Lou asked, confused.

He flashed that expensive-looking grin in her direction. "You said I could show up whenever. I came to check on Meatball."

Lou didn't know why having gotten a cat from Sebastian felt like she was being unfaithful to Noah, but the cats had always been their thing together. And even though she'd just gotten Meatball the other day, she felt like it might seem like she was hiding her from Noah. She just hadn't gotten around to asking him to do an exam. Getting a cat from Sebastian wasn't the same as when they found one on the street. Meatball had already gone to a vet and was completely up to date on her shots. Sebastian had given her all the paperwork to prove so.

And while Noah wasn't the jealous type, he definitely seemed confused.

"Meatball?" Noah glanced at her as if to ask about the name, cat names being something Lou had been quite vocal about in the past. "No literary name?" he asked instead.

"Actually, it's a cute story." She laughed uncomfortably, motioning for Sebastian to tell the story.

He cleared his throat. "I found her in an alley in the city, and she had a meatball in her mouth."

Noah arched an eyebrow. "Gotcha."

"Come in," Lou said, ushering them inside as she unlocked the bookshop.

Sebastian immediately strode over to a bookshelf where Sapphire and Charles Lickens were basking in the sunshine streaming through the front window. "Cats everywhere you look," he said with a chuckle. "I feel perfectly at home here." He beamed at Anne Mice and Catnip Everdeen, who were asleep on the couch in the middle of the shop.

Lou pulled the door shut and locked it, not wanting to add customers to the confusing mix, if she could help it. She rushed to the office, scooped up Meatball, and brought her out to where the two men stood in the middle of her bookshop. Noah held out his hands, gesturing for her to hand over the feline.

She did so, explaining to Sebastian, "Noah's the local veterinarian. He and I work together to find homes for the foster cats here."

"But not Meatball, right?" Sebastian asked.

"You're *keeping* her?" Noah asked, blurting out the question before he could stop himself.

Lou's gaze shot from him to Sebastian, then back to Noah. "She's had a really rough go of it. And she doesn't like men." Lou swallowed, seeing at that moment that Meatball had no issue being held by Noah. "Most of the time."

"Wow. That's amazing." Sebastian ran a hand through his thick brown hair. "She's never let me hold her like that. You have the magic touch, for sure."

Noah scratched behind her ears as she purred. "I can do an exam right now, if you'd like."

"She just had a checkup with my vet last week," Sebastian said.

"Who's your vet?" Noah asked.

Sebastian pushed back his shoulders. "A private one. She comes to my house to take care of the many cats I keep."

The tension between the two men was building in the room like humidity on a hot summer day. A loud meow came from upstairs. Catticus. He was still quarantined away from the tall bookshelves. As much as Lou appreciated the break in tension, Lou hated that he had to stay locked away from his friends.

"Who's that?" Sebastian asked.

"One of the rescue cats pulled a ligament, and he's on light physical activity until he heals," Lou explained.

"How'd he do that?" Sebastian asked.

"He's a bit of a daredevil," Noah said, setting Meatball

on the floor and letting her wander away. "Got his claw stuck while he was falling and couldn't release it in time."

Sebastian tsked. "Daredevil, huh?" He smiled. "Want to swap him for Meat?"

"Swap?" Noah practically choked out the word.

Lou considered the suggestion. "Actually, it's not a terrible idea. You should see his place, Noah. There are ropes, perches, and tons of places for Catticus to climb and jump. Safe places, not bookshelves. He'd be in heaven at Sebastian's. And there are a bunch of other cats there to keep him company."

Noah's jaw clenched, but he nodded.

"But Catticus has to get better first," Lou told Sebastian. "Maybe we'll try it once he gets the okay from Dr. Ramero here."

"Sounds good," Sebastian said. "Well, let me know if you need anything else." He turned to leave.

"Did you hear from your PI yet?" she asked before he could go.

"He's the one who told me about the blog post. Other than that, he hasn't come up with anything else yet. When he does, you'll be the first person I call." Sebastian winked. When he opened the front door to the bookshop, he took a moment to look up and down Thread Lane. "You were right, Lou. It's good for me to get out more." And with that, he left.

Noah waited until Sebastian's car pulled away before he set down Meatball and asked, "What's his PI going to tell him?"

"Oh." Lou exhaled a laugh, forgetting that Noah didn't

know about everything that had happened since she'd last seen him. "He's helping us with Vicki's case."

"You've been working with him?" Noah asked. It wasn't accusatory, but the earnestness behind his words made it clear that the answer was important.

"He was an investor in Vicki's company," Lou explained.

"Then he's a suspect in her death." Noah's expression turned dark, filled with worry.

"He has an alibi." Lou pursed her lips.

"Rich people can hire someone to do that kind of thing for them," Noah mumbled.

"Yes, but an investment like that is a drop in the bucket for someone like Sebastian," Lou countered. "He said it would cost exponentially more than that to have her killed."

Noah shot her a scowl. "The fact that he knows that is concerning."

"I'm sure he was guessing," Lou said, hoping she was right. "The point is, Sebastian gave me a list of the other investors, but he also mentioned that we shouldn't be looking at investors. Someone who was supposed to get half, or even a percentage of the money they scammed out of people, would have a much larger motivation to get Vicki out of the way."

"You think she was working with someone?" Noah asked.

Lou dipped her head in confirmation. "Well, again, it was Sebastian's idea. He said she was really good, had done her research about the area. He thought there might be a second or even third person involved in the scam. George and I asked around yesterday, and we have two leads. Apparently, Vicki spent a lot of time with James at the bank, and Nikki mentioned seeing a mysterious man hanging around town about a month before Vicki showed up."

"What did the man look like?" Noah asked, excitement flashing behind his brown eyes.

Lou relayed the description Nikki had given her yesterday. "I was going to stay closed today so George and I could ask around to see if anyone else has any other leads."

"I can help," Noah said.

Lou blinked. "Right now? Do you have time?"

"Yes," he answered with a smile.

"But what about the quilt convention?" she asked. *Or, more importantly, what about the feelings I have for you but haven't figured out how to talk to you about just yet?* Lou added in her thoughts.

"Don't worry about it," he told her. "It's not open just yet, but I'll make time."

As Lou was contemplating Noah's offer, her phone buzzed with a text from George.

> Dude. How's it going over there? It looks tense. Need an intervention?

When she glanced up, George was practically glued to the coffee shop window as she watched them.

Realizing she hadn't responded to Noah after he'd said he wanted to help her with the case, Lou said, "Um, let me just see if George minds." Typing out a reply, Lou sent the message.

> We're fine. Noah wants to help with the
> Vicki case. Is that okay with you?

She almost wished George would say no, giving Lou a reason not to have to spend the day with Noah. Putting off the conversation she needed to have with him until after the case was solved had sounded great in theory, but she hadn't anticipated Noah being by her side while she worked on Vicki's case. George was no help on that front, however. In fact, she automatically made things worse. She texted a response.

> It's probably better if we split up. I'll search
> the east side of town, and you and Noah
> hit the west.

Lou inwardly sighed, resigned to the fact that George was going to make her figure out Noah on her own.

> Meet later to discuss what we find?

Lou watched as George received the message. She sent back a thumbs-up.

> Good luck.

"Okay," Lou said to Noah. "George is taking the east side of town. We've got the west side."

Noah nodded seriously, adopting such a focused expression that Lou almost wanted to laugh. Almost. The complicated, unspoken conversation hanging between them quashed any humor she felt.

Looking around for Meatball, Lou found her surrounded by the shop cats. "Oh, whoops," Lou said. "I forgot to tell you I hadn't introduced her to them yet."

Noah cringed and rushed over, scooping her up once more. "She looks like she'd be fine, but since we're going to be gone, I'll put her back in the office."

Once Meatball was taken care of, they headed out on foot, making sure to leave a sign on the door letting customers know the bookshop would be closed all day. She and Noah walked in silence for about a block.

"The quilt convention is always full of people," Noah offered. He checked his watch. "But that doesn't open until nine. What about starting with Bea?" Noah motioned across the street to the Upholstered Button, the town's boutique furniture store.

The owner was definitely someone in the know. They crossed Yard Road, heading for the shop. Bea was just turning the sign in the front window to show that the store was now open.

"Welcome, you two." Bea opened the door and ushered them inside, smiling along with her greeting.

Something about how she said "you two," or maybe it was how she was smirking as she watched them enter, made Lou bristle with discomfort. Her words held a definite *look at how cute you are together* vibe. And even though that was what Lou desperately wanted, she needed to hold off on any conversations about "them" until after Silas was in the clear.

Lou put a little more space between herself and Noah as they stopped in the entryway. "Morning, Bea."

"What can I help you with?" she asked, staying put

instead of walking farther into the shop, as if she could already tell that the two weren't there for furniture.

"We're trying to help Silas by investigating the murder of Vicki Younger, and we have a few questions." Noah hooked his thumbs in his pockets. "You wouldn't know if there was anyone else working with Vicki?"

"As part of her 'business'?" Bea asked, using finger quotes around the last word.

Lou nodded, but added, "Though, we're not sure that they would've wanted us to know they were working together. This person might've been hanging around before Vicki showed up, casing the town." Lou used Sebastian's wording.

Bea blinked in surprise, like she hadn't thought about that before. "Oh, that's concerning." A frown marred her face. "Um, no one who I noticed."

"I'm guessing it would've been a man," Lou added, using the logic that if the partner really had killed Vicki, and the medical examiner had mentioned the size of the strangler's hands, it would be more likely to be a man. Plus, the person Nikki had described had been a man, though Lou didn't put too much stock in that since it was just one person.

Bea tipped her head to one side. "Now that you mention it, there was a man in here a few months ago. He struck me as odd because he looked like he was more fit for a beach town than the Pacific Northwest."

Excitement built in Lou.

Noah must've felt it, too, because he took a step forward. "How so?"

"He wore flip-flops, shorts, and a surf T-shirt," Bea said.

"Was he young?" Lou asked, not wanting to feed her any information.

Bea chuckled. "Not at all. He had a full white beard, wore sunglasses, and was almost completely bald."

That sounded just like the guy Nikki had described. They might really be onto something, Lou realized.

"And he hung around a lot?" Noah asked.

Bea squinted one eye. "I mean, not a lot. But he mentioned he wanted to move here and asked about the town and the county. I mentioned him to Smitty, and he said he'd stopped by the antique store as well, asking all the same questions."

Lou and Noah shared a look. They were on a roll. This definitely sounded like the kind of person Vicki might've sent ahead to scout out the town.

"Great." Lou smiled. "Thanks. We'll ask around about him."

Bea's thoughtful expression morphed into one of discomfort, like she'd just realized she had a rock in her shoe.

"What?" Noah narrowed his eyes at her.

"I'm not sure how much information you'll get out of locals today. In fact, I'm guessing they're going to be guarded for a while." Bea rubbed at her arm.

"Because of Vicki's murder?" Lou asked.

Bea shook her head. "At least a dozen people complained to me in the last twelve hours that they've seen things posted on the *BSB* blog that they swear they either never told anyone or only told their best friends," Bea said. "It's a bit panicky out there."

That matched with what George had told Lou that

morning. And while Lou had read through the piece about Sebastian, she hadn't checked the other recent entries on the blog.

"Do you think the *BSB* is paying people for town secrets?" Noah asked.

Bea and Lou shook their heads in tandem.

Noah looked surprised that Lou was weighing in.

"George came to me this morning, worried I was the *BSB* because we were the only two people who knew Sebastian Andrade was the man on the hill until today." Lou frowned. "And now it's on the blog."

"Maybe it's George?" Noah suggested.

Lou cut the air with her hand. "Why would she accuse me, then? She seemed genuinely confused."

"Looks like we have yet another mystery to solve." Noah looked at Bea, holding up a hand in goodbye. "Thank you for the information, Bea."

Noah and Lou started toward the door. They wandered up the street, not heading in any particular direction as they discussed what they'd learned.

"That's interesting about the *BSB*," Noah said, his brows furrowing as he thought.

"How else could they be getting gossip about people only a few people know?" Lou asked, choosing that part of the mystery to focus on.

But when she turned toward Noah to see what he thought, he was already pulling Lou into the alley behind Bea's shop.

He placed a hand on the small of her back. Leaning in close, he whispered, "There's a man following us."

CHAPTER 15

As much as she wanted to, Lou didn't turn around or try to peek around the corner right away. Noah's eyes shifted between her and the street in worry.

"What does the man following us look like?" she asked.

"Blond hair. Kind of jittery. Beard." Noah wiggled his fingers toward his chin.

Lou huffed in disappointment. It wasn't the old beach-bum man Bea or Nikki had described. With that option out of the question, Lou peered around the building, leaving the safety of Noah's side, though his fingers remained secure around her arm. Sure enough, a man with a light brown beard and fluffy blond hair shot glances in their direction from where he pretended to be checking out the local newspaper box.

Just because this man didn't fit the description they'd gotten from Bea and Nikki, didn't mean he couldn't still be involved in Vicki's death.

Lou may have been afraid, but she was also a New Yorker—well, an honorary one, after living there for two decades. Whirling around the building, Lou felt her arm slip through Noah's protective grasp. She strode toward the blond man so quickly, he didn't have time to react.

"Do we have a problem here?" she asked in her best New York accent.

He put both of his hands up, as if she carried a gun along with her fake accent. "No. I... This... No." He shook his head emphatically, taking a step away from her.

Noah was next to Lou in a second. "Why are you following us?"

The man stammered for another few seconds. "It's my job," he finally spat out. "I'm a private investigator. Wesley Saint James, nice to meet you." He held out a hand, but neither Noah nor Lou shook it. "Okaaay," he said, using the hand he'd been holding out to smooth through his hair, like he was some kind of blond Fonzie character.

Lou narrowed her eyes. Private investigator? "Wait. Are you Sebastian Andrade's PI?" Lou asked. When he nodded, she added, "What are you doing following *us*?"

At her question, he glanced at his shoes and said, "I-uh-well, I wasn't getting anywhere in Brine, so I thought I'd follow you since Sebastian said you seemed, and I quote, 'as smart as you are beautiful.'" The young man cocked an eyebrow suggestively at Lou.

Lou purposefully didn't look at Noah after that, but out of the corner of her eye, she thought she saw him clench his jaw.

"So you didn't find any leads about a business associate in Brine?" Lou asked, hoping to move the conversation back toward the case.

"Believe me. I live there. And all they've done is harp on

and on about how it was probably someone in Button who'd killed Vicki." His tone was bored and sarcastic.

Lou checked her watch. It was almost time for the quilt convention to start. She and Noah needed to head in that direction. "Okay, well, since you're here … I'm going to give you a lead to follow."

Wesley's bored expression lit up. "Sure."

Noah looked less than certain when she finally chanced a glance in his direction, but she took his silence as a sign that she should continue.

"We've heard there was a man who was hanging around about a month prior to Vicki showing up in town." Lou described the older man just as Bea and Nikki had. "We have someplace to be, but I want you to search the town, ask if anyone's seen him lately."

Wesley inhaled, puffing out his chest. "You've got it."

She held out her hand. "Give me your phone, and I'll put my number in it. Text me if you see or hear anything."

Wesley did as she said, and they parted ways. Noah was quiet for a few minutes after that, not saying much other than offering to drive them to the convention. Lou couldn't be sure if he was upset about what Sebastian had said about her or if he was still on alert after thinking they were being followed maliciously.

Lou didn't push him, though, and he loosened up by the time they'd arrived at the park. He seemed back to his normal self once they stepped foot inside the quilting convention tent. Cricket eyed them from behind her button booth, arching an eyebrow suggestively. Lou shook her head as discreetly as possible, trying to communicate that she hadn't talked to Noah yet.

The older woman pouted but seemed to drop the subject as she turned to talk to a customer.

"Where should we start?" Noah asked, none the wiser about the communication that had passed between Lou and his honorary aunt.

Lou scanned the space. She pointed to the nearest booth. "How about here, and we can work our way around?"

Noah nodded, and they walked over to the man selling rotary cutters. Neither he nor the next seven booth owners had seen a man with a white beard and flip-flops anywhere near the quilting convention.

Lou was losing hope when her phone buzzed with an incoming text message. It was from Wesley.

> Are you sure your old man was wearing
> flip-flops? I found one who's acting
> suspicious around the bank, but he has
> leather loafers on instead.

Showing the text to Noah, Lou typed an excited response.

> Maybe he changed it up because he knew
> what we would look for. What else can you
> tell me about the old man you're
> watching?

Lou and Noah moved away from the booths while they waited for Wesley to respond. They read the text together when it came through.

He's wearing a bowler hat and has really fluffy eyebrows. Looks like he might grumble a lot, possibly at kids to get off his lawn.

"Oh," Noah said. Disappointment leaked from his posture. "It's just Silas."

But Lou couldn't be let down. She was too busy being mad. "I told him to stay at Button House. Why can't that man listen to a single—" She stopped herself, placing the back of her hand onto her forehead to help her calm down. "He needs to leave, or he could get himself in real trouble. It looks like I'm needed at the bank."

"Want company?" Noah asked, but even as he did so, she could see him focusing in on different things that could use his attention around the tent.

"Thank you, but I can handle Silas," she said. "You stay here and help your family. Thank you for your help this morning."

Though confusing, it had been nice to spend time with Noah. She vowed to have a conversation with him soon. It just wasn't the time.

As if her worried thoughts had been written on her face, Noah said, "Oh, you don't have your car, do you? Take my truck." He pulled out his keys and placed them in her hand. "I can get a ride back from one of my family members. Just let me know where you park it."

"Thanks," Lou said, a little sad that he'd misinterpreted what she'd actually been bothered about. "I'll let you know how it goes with Silas." She broke into a jog back toward the parking lot.

Pulling into the bank parking lot a few minutes later, it

took Lou a moment to locate Wesley or Silas. Then she spotted a shock of fluffy blond hair just before Wesley ducked back down in the driver's seat of a Honda Civic. She walked over to the car, knocking on the window.

Wesley let out a yelp, but then calmed down when he saw it was her. "You scared the change out of my pocket, lady."

"Lou." She crossed her arms. "Not *lady*."

He rolled his eyes. "Fine. Lou, didn't anyone teach you not to sneak up on people?" Wesley held up his phone and tapped the screen. "And to text people back?"

She grimaced. "Sorry." She'd completely forgotten to answer his last text.

"I've been waiting to go confront this guy. Do you think it's the one you heard people talking about?" Wesley's gaze wandered back toward the edge of the parking lot, where Lou spotted Silas only partially hidden behind one of the bushes next to the small forest.

Lou shook her head. "While it's not the man we're looking for, I need to get him back to his assisted-living complex. Thanks for alerting me about him. You can keep searching for the other old man."

With that, she stormed over to Silas, who saw her coming and swore under his breath before moving a branch to block his face.

"I can see you," she deadpanned, placing her hands on her hips.

He glanced over each of his shoulders. "Who?"

"Silas, I told you to stay home. What are you doing?" Lou looked up at the sky for a moment as she tried to keep her frustration in check.

He peered out from behind the leaves. "I saw the beekeeper again. I had to come check it out."

She closed her eyes for a moment as she gathered her strength. "What?"

"Like I told you about the day I was following Vicki, I saw a beekeeper driving a car," he explained, then yanked her into the bush with him. "Shhh. There he is."

Lou swatted branches and leaves out of her way as she got her bearings and turned herself around. Once she'd untangled her arms from the bush, she peered out in the direction Silas stared. A man in shorts, a surf T-shirt, and flip-flops was circling the bank. He had a white beard and a bald head.

From his car, Wesley pointed animatedly at the man.

"It's him." She blinked at Silas in surprise. "You found him."

Puffing out his chest, Silas beamed for a moment before asking. "Who? Did you see the beekeeper driving by too?"

But Lou didn't have time to answer him. The old man was about to disappear around the other side of the bank. She broke free from the bush and raced after him. A car door slammed to her right, and she was vaguely aware that Wesley was coming with her.

"Hey," she called to the older man. "I need to talk to you."

She couldn't see his eyes behind the sunglasses, but his eyebrows popped up in surprise at the sight of her, Wesley, and Silas, too.

With no hesitation, the man broke into a run, disappearing around the bank.

Eyes narrowing, Lou followed, wishing she'd worn her

running shoes rather than sandals. But at least she had more support than the old man. She could hear his flimsy footwear slapping against his heels as he ran, the sound echoing off the brick exterior walls of the bank.

He hadn't gotten very far by the time she rounded the corner.

"Stop," she called. "I just want to talk."

He kept running even as she gained on him. Knowing she didn't want to tackle the guy, she swung wide around the corner and blocked him from running into the woods.

"Stop."

He finally did, panting, but his eyes were still swiveling in discomfort.

A few moments later, Wesley came screeching around the building. "Dude, you're fast," he said to Lou, then turned his attention toward the man. "You're not. Flip-flops, my dude?" He tutted.

Finally, Silas rounded the corner, and they were all together.

"What do you all want?" the flip-flop man asked.

"You knew Vicki, didn't you?" Lou asked, backing the question with the same amount of New York boldness she'd used with Wesley earlier, sans the fake accent.

The man let his shoulders slump forward in defeat. He nodded as he continued to pant for air.

"Were you her business partner?" Lou guessed, knowing that was a bit of a leap, but she wanted to understand who he was and how he was connected to the case.

He gulped. "Who are you? The police?" His frantic eyes moved over her as if searching for a badge.

She shook her head, but realized she probably shouldn't

let him know how unprepared she was to meet up with a potential murderer. "I'm a local investigator, though." She curled her fingers around Noah's truck keys just in case she needed to use one as a small stabbing implement in defense.

To her surprise, the old man said, "I'm Todd. Yes, I was working with Vicki." He looked over his shoulders before adding, "but I don't really feel like it at this point. She obviously didn't fill me in on a few important details of the job, and she stole all the money, hiding it away somewhere I can't find, before she was offed."

"You weren't the one to hurt her?" Lou asked, even though she knew it was a rather audacious question.

He scoffed. "Absolutely not. In fact, it would be great if you can help me. I think I'm next."

CHAPTER 16

L ou blinked. "What do you mean, you're next?" She took a step closer to Todd. "Wait, do you know who killed Vicki?"

Todd wet his lips. "I have no idea. All I know is that we were being followed, and then she's gone, but I'm still seeing that beekeeper suit everywhere I look." The man seemed unhinged. His mannerisms were manic, and he kept looking over his shoulder.

"Wait. What did you just say about a beekeeper?" Lou asked, having heard Silas say the same thing.

Before Todd could answer her, Silas stormed past her, closing in on Todd. "Yeah, tell us now. This is getting blamed on me. What did you do to her?"

Lou shot a pleading look at Wesley. "Can you take this one away from here?" She motioned to Silas. "I'd like to talk to Todd alone." Lou didn't really want to, but she also didn't want to lose him.

Once she and Todd were alone, Lou asked, "Why do you think the beekeeper means you're in danger?" An icy feeling moved over her skin. She'd dismissed Silas's beekeeper comments as nonsense, but what if they'd been an important clue she and Roy had overlooked?

"The answer is on the bottom of your sandal." He pointed to Lou's right shoe.

She glanced down. "What?"

"Give me your sandal. I'll show you." Todd nodded earnestly.

Lou frowned, but she kept her eyes on him as she reached down and slipped her right sandal off her foot. She turned it over but didn't see anything. She handed it over.

Todd looked at it as if he were studying it for a split second before he chucked it about half a football field behind her. Then he ran.

Lou groaned in frustration as he disappeared into the woods behind the bank. "Lou, how'd you fall for that?" she asked herself as she hopped on one foot back toward where Todd had thrown her shoe. Wesley and Silas peered around the building, looking at her with confused interest and then looking at the shoe. Seeing her hopping, Wesley raced over and grabbed her sandal.

"Do you want me to run after him?" Wesley asked as he handed Lou her sandal. "Or maybe you should."

Embarrassment crept over her. She couldn't believe she'd been duped like that. She'd been living in a small town for too long, she realized. New York City Lou would've smacked her upside the head after falling for that.

"No," she said dejectedly. "I'm going to let the professionals handle it now."

Wesley jabbed his thumb at his chest in question before he noticed her grabbing her phone.

She called Roy.

"Hello?" he answered warily.

"Roy, I just met Vicki's *business partner*." She laced the words with sarcasm. "But I lost him in the woods."

"On my way," he said quickly. "Where are you?"

"The bank." She hung up and glared at Silas. "You're going home, and I want you to take him," she told Wesley. "He lives at Button House, up the road. Make sure he gets there safely."

Silas and Wesley opened their mouths at the same time as if they would protest, but Lou snapped her fingers.

"Silas, Roy is on his way," she said. "Do you really want him to find you here?" She placed a hand on her hip.

The old man shook his head.

"And, Wesley, in your experience, how do cops feel about private investigators?" she asked. "Because I can tell you that *Detective* Roy Anderson won't be thrilled that I'm working on this case, but he'll be a lot less happy to find you here."

Wesley's gaze darkened with worry. She had him there.

"Get Silas home, and then come back here to watch the bank. Make sure Todd doesn't come back this way. Okay?" She waited until the two men nodded in concession.

Wesley and Silas muttered excuses but walked toward Button House.

Lou sighed and tried to take a few deep breaths before Roy pulled up in his sedan a few minutes later. She leaned into the passenger side window as he rolled it down.

"He ran back toward where I found Vicki." Lou motioned to the forest.

Roy pulled into the bank lot and parked somewhat

haphazardly in the first open space. He got out, rushing toward the trees. Lou followed.

"What are you doing?" he asked, coming to a stop.

"Coming with you." When Roy sent her a tired glare, she added, "I don't think Todd's the murderer. He talked about how he and Vicki were being followed, and he thinks he might be next." She groaned. "Roy, we're wasting time. I can help you since I know what he looks like."

Detective Anderson grunted out a single syllable that Lou assumed to be the word "Fine" since he didn't stop her from following this time as he stalked off down the small footpath into the woods. She jogged to keep up with his long strides.

"So how do you know this guy was Vicki's business partner?" Roy growled out the question after they'd been walking for a few yards. The tightness to his tone told Lou he and his team hadn't yet discovered that Vicki had been working with anyone.

"Well, the thing is..." Lou left the sentence hanging, warring with the need to make him feel better by letting him know it hadn't been her idea, either, and the worry that he'd be upset that she'd brought *more* people on the case. Since he already seemed quite upset with her, and she was bad at lying, she decided to spill everything. "I talked to one of the investors, Sebastian Andrade, who brought up the fact that she was too good of a con artist for this to be her first time, or for her to be working alone." Lou shrugged. "So we started asking around about a man who might've come to scout out the town before she got here."

"And you found him?" Roy's tone lifted as if she'd genuinely impressed him.

"With some help," Lou said, a little uncomfortable with the amount of credit he seemed to assign to Lou in his mind. "And don't be too awed. I had him, but he fooled me in a *very* embarrassing way." Lou ducked under a branch as they walked into the clearing where Vicki's car had been parked just under a week ago.

Where Lou had found her body.

It was empty now: no car and no Todd either.

Roy chuckled, catching Lou off guard as they kept walking. "I think I need to hear how he fooled you," Roy said, reminding Lou of what she'd said just before being surprised by the scene of the crime. "For the prosperity of the case, of course," Roy added, clearing his throat.

"He fooled me by telling me there was something on the bottom of my shoe." Her tone was one long groan.

"And then he threw it, didn't he?" Roy guessed.

Lou hid her face with her hands before she nodded in confirmation. "He knew I was faster than him. Plus, the man was wearing flip-flops."

Roy stopped short. "Like that?" He pointed to a black flip-flop, about two yards to their right, just like Todd had been wearing. It was stuck in a bush, like it had flown off his foot while he was running.

"Exactly." Lou surged forward. "Todd." She cupped her fingers around her mouth as she called into the small collection of trees. "We can help you. Please, just talk to us."

They walked forward, calling out his name as a small ravine appeared to the right of the trail, a creek cutting through the brush at the bottom. Lou scanned the space, looking for his white T-shirt or his khaki shorts.

To her utter dismay, she spotted both at the bottom of the small ravine.

"Todd." The name was an exhale as Lou took off running down the banks of the creek, picking her way through the brush as carefully as she could.

Roy followed her, surging ahead since he was wearing shoes instead of sandals like her. He reached Todd first, picking up the man's wrist to check for a pulse. But Lou didn't need to wait for Roy to shake his head to confirm that Todd was dead.

Even though he lay on his stomach, his face was pointed toward her, and his eyes were open. The collar of his T-shirt was low enough that Lou could see the red marks just appearing around his neck.

Roy swore under his breath as he pulled out his phone. "I'm gonna need backup. Out near where we found the first victim. Another body, same cause of death. Male. Probably sixties or seventies. Thank you." He slid his phone back into his pocket and sighed as he stood.

Guilt washed over Lou. "I just saw him. If I hadn't fallen for the shoe thing—" she cut out, her voice getting too wobbly with emotion.

"Hey." Roy strode toward her and placed a hand on her arm. "He ran away from you. You couldn't have known."

The surprising show of kindness from the ornery detective jolted Lou out of her self-pity. Roy seemed to realize what he was doing, and he stepped back too.

"At least Silas was nowhere near *this* guy right before he died," Roy said, possibly still trying to make her feel better.

But it didn't. Lou cringed.

Roy exhaled a tired breath. "You can't be serious."

Lou knew he would find out eventually, so she didn't even bother lying to protect Silas. "He was the one who helped me find Todd." Lou pointed to the man next to the creek. "I made him go back to Button House right before I called you, though. There's an eyewitness, and I'm sure he'll show up on the security cameras there before this happened." She grimaced at Todd's body.

Roy glanced over his shoulder as sirens grew closer to the forest. "The killer is probably still somewhere in these woods." He looked up as cruisers pulled to a stop in the clearing near them. Once the officers spilled out, he directed them to, "Fan out and search the woods."

The reality sent a shiver through Lou even though there wasn't a hint of cold in the air. The killer had been two steps ahead of her. Was Todd their final victim or were they just getting started?

CHAPTER 17

L ou kept it together long enough to answer Detective Anderson's questions about Todd, telling Roy everything, even details that seemed silly or insignificant before. She shared all about their trip to see Francis and Sebastian, everything Todd had said to her, even the odd bit about the beekeeper.

But once Detective Anderson released her from the crime scene, sending an officer to walk back with her to the bank parking lot, Lou's fingers began shaking and any noise in the woods made her jump. Maybe it was because it was the second body she'd seen that week, or maybe it was how close she must've been to the killer, but fear curled around her, making it hard to breathe.

When they reached the parking lot, Lou looked around for Wesley. He must've taken her comments about the detective's feelings toward private investigators seriously because he and the car he'd been sitting in were gone.

Next she scanned the parking lot for her car, but couldn't find it. It was then that she remembered she'd driven Noah's truck. She pulled out her phone. He'd already texted about ten minutes ago.

How'd everything go with Silas?

Right. She was supposed to update him. Swallowing, she considered how to summarize everything that had happened into a text.

Sorry. Things got complicated.

She sent that message first, hoping it might prepare him for what was coming next. But as she typed and erased multiple messages, she decided there wasn't a good way to put what had happened in a text. She settled on just the basics.

Found Silas. He's back at Button House, safe and sound. Thanks for the use of your truck. Do you want me to bring it back to you?

Even as she typed the message, Lou could see that Noah was already typing a response. His texts came through in quick succession after hers.

That's good.

Why don't you just take my truck to your place?

I have to help my dad and might be late,
so you can just hide the keys in the
jasmine planter to the right of the
bookshop. That way I can grab it whenever
without having to wake you.

Lou sent him a message telling him she'd do just that. As much as she wanted to assure him she could stay up and wait for him to stop by, she was already feeling the fatigue of the day settle over her. She could fill him in on everything that happened tomorrow.

Climbing into Noah's truck, Lou drove it to the bookshop and tucked his keys into the planter, covering them with one of the green leaves. With that, she headed inside, falling asleep the moment her head hit her pillow, even before the sun had fully set.

The next morning, Noah's truck was gone when Lou woke. He'd sent her a message after eleven telling her he'd picked it up. Regardless of the extra sleep she'd gotten, Lou still couldn't seem to let her mind or fears settle.

Being in her cozy bookshop with the cats helped, as did being back in her routine, but she was still feeling all sorts of melancholy when closing time came around that evening. Meatball was actually a big help, showing Lou all the affection she could ever hope to receive from a cat. Sapphire was sweet and showed his affection often by curling up next to her on the couch or rubbing his face against her when he wanted to give her extra attention. But he'd been with her since he was a tiny kitten. He'd known nothing other than a warm house and loving owners.

Meatball knew what it was like to be alone, scared, and hungry. And she seemed to want Lou to know just how much she appreciated her. Sebastian had definitely been right about her preferring females. Immediately, she seemed more comfortable in Lou's company than she had in Sebastian's. Lou's only lingering worry had been the male customers in her bookshop. Meatball didn't seem to mind them as long as Lou was around, but she still cowered and crouched behind a bookshelf until they left.

"As much as I'd like to keep you, I think it might be better if we can find a home for you where you won't ever have to deal with men again." Lou wondered if such a place existed.

When she closed for the day, she felt too jittery and nervous to stay put in her apartment and read, like she normally might have. Going on a run by herself didn't seem like a good idea either. She wanted Willow to have fun but couldn't wait until she got home. About to call George to see what she was up to that evening, Lou remembered the quilt convention. She'd gone with Noah yesterday, but that had been part of a mission to find out information. She just needed to go as a tourist, not be focused on the case any longer. There were tons of people there and plenty for her to browse through.

She moved the cats upstairs, grabbed her purse, and headed for the park.

Although Lou had every intention of shopping and losing herself in the crowds, her feet took her directly to Cricket's button booth. Either Cricket had heard what happened yesterday—something Lou wouldn't be surprised about in this town—or Lou just looked *that* awful, but the woman jumped out of her chair and pulled Lou into a tight hug the moment she locked her gaze on her.

Lou sank into the embrace, feeling tears crowding her eyes. Vicki's death had been sad, of course, but Lou couldn't help but take Todd's harder since she'd seen him alive just minutes before he'd died. She'd probably been the last person he talked to. Unless … Lou shivered as she thought of the killer and what they might've said to him before they strangled him.

Cricket led Lou around the booth and sat her down in one of her chairs, rubbing her back. "There's nothing you could've done, my dear." Her voice was soothing and loosened some of the tightness in Lou's lungs. "Has Noah ever told you about my superpower?"

Lou smirked through her worry, like the sun breaking through thick clouds. "He neglected to fill me in. What's your superpower?"

"I can tell you what fabric anyone reminds me of." She pushed back her shoulders and raised her chin with pride.

"Is that so?" Lou asked.

"Take Rosa," Cricket said, mentioning Noah's mother. "She's a seasonal cotton print, like the ones they keep near the front of Material Girls."

"Because she's there to greet customers right when they arrive?" Lou guessed.

"And because she's bright, complex, and puts a smile on your face, no matter who you are," Cricket explained. "Carlos is like the hardy indoor-outdoor fabric they keep on the back wall at the store. It's almost indestructible, weathered, and strong. That man is content to let the women run the place, but as a former handyman, he keeps the shop looking nice, making new shelves or tables when they're needed. He's an unassuming, supportive kind of person."

Lou beamed at the description of Noah's father. As she'd gotten to know him around town, she had to agree. He wasn't only funny and kind, but she could see so many of his exceptional qualities in Noah, not to mention his penchant for helping people.

"What about Paloma?" Lou asked, arching an eyebrow. Noah's grandmother was a force to be reckoned with.

"Silk," Cricket answered without pause. "Smooth, strong, goes with the flow, and she makes everyone feel fancier just being around her."

Lou grinned. She couldn't argue with that. She also couldn't argue with Cricket's method of taking her mind off her worries. Her hands no longer shook, and she felt almost relaxed after the distraction.

Either Cricket thought Lou still needed more calming down, or she was merely on a roll, because she kept going. "Bianca and Elena are as different as can be," Cricket said with a chuckle as she mentioned Noah's aunts.

"I think I'm getting the hang of this." Lou squinted one eye. "Bianca has to be fleece, right?" she asked, mentioning the cozy, incredibly soft fabric they kept near the back of the store. "It's inviting and so nice to hug, just like Bianca."

Cricket nodded emphatically. "You've got it."

"Elena, though." Lou clicked her tongue. "She's…"

"Complicated. Multilayered. Serious. Like brocade," Cricket finally supplied when she could see Lou wasn't going to guess that one.

Lou snapped her fingers.

"What about Noah?" Cricket asked.

Lou couldn't help the weightlessness that took over whenever she thought of him. "Flannel, for sure. Sturdy, but soft. Just what you want wrapped around you on a chilly night." Lou slapped her hand over her mouth as the words left her lips.

Cricket tipped her head back in a delighted cackle. "It's okay, darling. We'll give you a pass on that subconscious slip. You've had a hard couple of days."

"Thanks," Lou said with a groan, wishing she could hop into one of the nearby lakes to get rid of the heat of embarrassment. "So, what fabric am *I*?" She stared at Cricket, searching her face for the answer.

Cricket studied Lou for a moment, but smiled as she said, "You're denim, like me. We're sturdy and comfortable and people can depend on us, but sometimes we're fraying at the edges, and people don't realize right away."

The immense weight on Lou's chest had lifted, and she could breathe deeply once more. "Thanks for distracting me."

"Anytime, sweetie." Cricket sent Lou a sidelong glance. "Any chance you want to talk about Noah, or why you haven't told him how you feel just yet? He's at the quilt shop right now, you know. Alone."

But before Lou could answer, a text came through from George that made Lou stand straight up.

"I have to go," she told Cricket as she reread the text.

> Meet me at the coffee shop ASAP. There's something you need to see.

George and Ruby were pacing in front of the Bean and Button when Lou pulled up and parked in front of the coffee shop. Lou jumped out of her car and raced over to meet them.

"What's going on?" Lou asked, concern growing as she took in the agitated state of the two women.

The coffee shop was closed, which wasn't unusual for that time in the evening, but Ruby kept glancing at it over her shoulder as if they'd trapped a gigantic spider inside, and they didn't want to have to go back and face it.

George's eyebrows were furrowed so tight, a deep groove sat in between them, marring her usually smooth forehead. Instead of answering Lou's question, George pulled out her phone and held it toward Lou, showing her a picture.

"What am I looking at?" Lou asked, rotating her head to the side. Was it a microchip?

George cleared her throat. "Inside the coffee shop, I found a recording device at the bottom of one of the napkin dispensers. Ruby didn't know it was there. We found three more throughout the coffee shop, but we're not sure if that's all of them." Even though the microphones were inside, George still barely talked above a whisper, as if she was worried she might be overheard.

Lou's eyes widened as she took in the information. "This could be how the *BSB* knows so much about the town secrets when no one told anyone."

"And how the *BSB* knew about Sebastian," George said. "We talked about him that day while we were sitting at the table where I found the first one. Sorry I accused you,"

George added on, giving Lou a small smile along with the apology.

"It's okay." Lou shot a concerned look at George and then Ruby. "I'm still confused about why you called me. This seems like something Roy should handle."

At that, Ruby arched her eyebrows at George, shooting her a scowl out of the corner of her eye. "Because George wants to keep the devices in my coffee shop for a little bit longer," Ruby scoffed, obviously not a fan of that idea.

George's lips peeled into a smile. "I can order a scanner to search for more throughout town, and then we could use it to our advantage and mess with the *BSB*, tell them a bunch of stuff that's not true and get them to post lies."

As much as Lou liked the idea of teaching whoever was behind the gossip blog a lesson not to listen in on people's conversations, she didn't want to add to the chaos.

"I think we need to let Roy handle it from here," Lou said. "I'll text him."

George seemed a little let down, her shoulders slumping forward in defeat, but she nodded. Ruby relaxed at Lou's suggestion. She likely didn't want those things in her coffee shop any longer than they'd already been there.

Lou sent the text to Roy.

> Hey, sorry to bug you.

Lou took a moment to laugh at her unintended pun.

I know you're busy, but George found recording devices hidden in the Bean and Button. We think the BSB has been using them to find out the townspeople's secrets. Can you send someone over to collect them and make sure there aren't any more?

Three dots appeared on the screen, then disappeared. They appeared again and disappeared. Roy must've been at a loss for words about the situation. Finally, an answer came through.

Wow. Creepy. Sending Officer Little.

Thanks.

"Officer Little's on his way," she said to Ruby and George.

But even though knowing the police were on their way should've calmed Lou down, she suddenly broke into a cold sweat.

She and George had discussed Sebastian Andrade in the coffee shop, but that hadn't been *all* they'd talked about in that location. The morning after their conversation about Sebastian, she'd confessed to having feelings for Noah, a tidbit the *BSB* hadn't published … at least, she didn't think they had.

"Sorry, I have to go." Lou spun on her heel and headed for her car, not even waiting for George or Ruby to say goodbye.

As she climbed into her car, worry moved up Lou's

arms, causing them to tingle and break out in goose bumps. The *BSB* could let the information about her feelings for Noah loose at any moment. She checked the site, glad to see there wasn't a post about them, but the worry roiling in her stomach told her she didn't want Noah to read it before she had the chance to talk to him. His family, not to mention his ex-wife, read that blog, and she felt awful that she may have said something that could make his life harder. She needed to give him a heads-up. Her plan to wait on having the conversation about her feelings with Noah was no longer an option. In fact, it seemed as if waiting had only made things more difficult.

Heading to the quilt shop, Lou gulped, having zero clue how she was going to tell Noah that she not only thought of him as more than a friend, but that she may have inadvertently shared that secret with the entire town.

CHAPTER 18

By the time she walked through the quilt shop's front door a few minutes later, Lou's nerves were in knots worse than the bundle of random wires she'd found in a box in the bookshop when she'd inherited it. Lou's stomach flipped as Noah glanced up and smiled at the sight of her. She hated the fact that what she had to tell him might make that grin disappear.

At least there didn't seem to be any customers in the store at the moment. *A small consolation*, Lou thought incredulously.

"Hey, do you have news about the case?" he asked.

Unlike his Aunt Cricket, Noah must *not* have heard the news about Todd just yet. It surprised her.

"Or … the cat?" Noah guessed, taking her silence as an answer that he'd gotten it wrong. "What was its name, again? Meatloaf?"

Lou couldn't help but burst out into laughter. "Meatball, and no. She's fine. I do have news about the case." The words, *but first,* were on the tip of her tongue. She knew she would lose her nerve if she didn't jump right in and tell him about the *BSB* and the listening devices the blogger had placed around the coffee shop.

Before she could say anything, however, he pulled her over to the tables full of pattern books sitting in the middle of the shop. "News? What happened?"

"I found Vicki's partner yesterday," Lou explained. "His name was Todd."

"What?" Noah blinked in disbelief. "Wait … *was?*"

Lou winced. "He … he didn't make it." She swallowed. "We found him dead too."

Noah's jaw clenched. "I'm so sorry."

Just as she always did in Noah's presence, Lou felt calmer. She grinned at the realization that he'd become just as safe of a person to her as Willow was. And while Willow being gone for an entire week might've made her feel such a hole in her life a year ago, she realized now that she had other people to turn to.

"We should tell Roy to look into whether Sebastian has an alibi for that death too," Noah said, catching Lou off guard.

Lou narrowed her eyes at him. "I already gave him Sebastian's name, but I really don't believe Sebastian had anything to do with this. What's your problem with him?" Lou asked carefully, genuinely curious. She didn't mean it accusatorially, and she hoped it didn't come out that way.

Noah's brown eyes met hers for a moment, and then he closed them with a sigh. "I'm sorry. I think I have trust issues with people like him." He blinked his eyes open and stared at her with sincerity. "I understand there are plenty of rich people who give back and help the community—

which it sounds like he's doing with the cats he's taking care of—but I came from a second-generation American family whose parents were immigrants. Stories about millionaires when I was growing up were all about greed and personal gain and corruption."

"I understand, but I think we need to trust Roy with that part of it." Lou fiddled with her keys as she contemplated what she was about to ask him. Nerves spiked in her gut and inside her chest, but she needed to talk to him. "Want to get dinner? Or do you have plans?"

"No plans. I'd love to grab some dinner." Noah patted his pockets. "I just need to lock up." He frowned as he continued to search, moving from his front pockets to the back ones. His gaze wandered over to the counter where a key ring sat. His face relaxed with understanding. "I forgot I loaned my shop key to my dad."

"Do you need to call him?" Lou asked, knowing they couldn't very well leave the shop unlocked.

"I know where Mom keeps a spare," Noah said, shaking his head.

He made his way over to the cutting counter, opening a drawer that had long tubes with buttons in each one. Someone had glued the type of button that was inside the tube to the top of the container. Noah extracted one with a shiny purple button glued on top. Inside, there weren't buttons, but a key.

Lou pointed to the container. "That's clever. It's like it hides in plain sight." Even though she was the one who said the sentence, it sent an idea jolting through her.

"What?" Noah asked, registering her change in demeanor.

"I was just thinking about the bank. Not only was Vicki hanging around, acting as if she was searching for something before she died, but that's where we found Todd too. He was sneaking around the building before he ran off." Lou gulped as she remembered what had happened to him there.

"You think Vicki hid something?" Noah cocked an eyebrow. "But if she hid it, why couldn't she find it?"

Lou pursed her lips. "Silas said she ran into the woods. Maybe she got interrupted by whoever Todd was sure was following them and ran away before she could recover whatever she left behind. Todd did say he thought a beekeeper was following them."

"A beekeeper? Just like Silas said." Noah's eyes sparkled with excitement. "Well, there's only one way to find out." He showed her to the door, locking it behind them and leading the way to his truck. The bank was closed, but that didn't matter since they wouldn't need to get inside.

Once they were parked, Lou jumped out, leaving her purse behind. She didn't want it to hinder her searching. She walked up to the bank and recited what Silas had told them.

"Remember, Silas said she circled the bank building three times." Lou chewed on her lip.

Noah snapped his fingers. "Maybe because she couldn't find what she was looking for."

Lou nodded. "And he said she was leaning in close like she was listening to the bricks as she kicked the walls."

"She was kicking the walls," Noah repeated as if he was really digesting the words, trying to see if they contained any hidden meaning.

Lou's eyes flicked open. "What if it wasn't the walls, but the bricks specifically?" She scanned the side of the building, rushing over to use her toe to test each of the bricks. "There could be a loose one."

"And she hid something behind the brick." Noah understood where Lou was going with her train of thought, and he joined her, kicking the toe of his shoe against the bottom three layers of bricks to test if any of them moved.

A few minutes later, they'd almost completely encircled the building and found no removable bricks. Lou swiped at her forehead, the evening heat getting to her after all the kicking.

"This is a very well-made building," Noah said, exhaling as he rested his palms against the bricks. "Not a single one of these even so much as wiggled."

Noah's comment reminded Lou that one brick *had* wiggled for her. She'd checked it, and it wouldn't come out, but maybe that wasn't the point. Maybe the wiggly brick signified something else. Silas had said Vicki had been clawing at the dirt. Vicki could've used the one slightly wiggly brick to mark where she'd buried something.

"She wasn't *listening* to the bricks, she was kicking them to check for the loose one." Lou stepped back, looking at the wall and trying to remember where that wobbly brick had been. There had been a rhododendron branch sticking into her back when she'd squatted down to see if it would come out. Lou looked for the rhododendrons, and something clicked.

About two weeks earlier, Willow had been complaining about those very plants.

"I know James and I have a history," she'd said. "But he

could've asked *me* to plant the new ones instead of someone else." Willow had glared at the plants native to the Pacific Northwest. "I own a nursery just up the road, after all."

Looking at Noah, Lou filled him in on what she was thinking. "James just recently hired a landscaper to add twice as many rhododendrons here. I think by adding more plants, he messed up Vicki's system to remember where she'd hidden something. That's why she had to go around the building so many times."

"That makes sense," Noah said. "So the first clue was the loose brick."

Lou wiggled her fingers as she thought. "The second could've had to do with the position of the plants. But she got messed up since there were twice as many after she was gone for a few weeks."

"She was digging in the dirt," Noah reminded her. "So she must've buried something."

Lou chewed on her lip as she thought. "She would've marked it." That was when her eyes caught on one of the pine cones that had been strewn about the place. She knelt and picked one up. Looking at Noah, she said, "How many pine cones do you see?"

He frowned. "Just these three."

A triangle. Lou made sure she was lined up with the wiggly brick, then she regarded the three pine cones. Walking forward until she was standing, roughly in the middle of all three, she checked the dirt. Under the new topsoil layer the landscaper had added, the dirt underneath was solid.

"Oh, wait. I found another pine cone here." Noah

stepped forward. "It's kind of covered by the soil, though." He bent to pick it up, but it wouldn't budge. "It's stuck."

Lou raced over, moving the mulch with her fingers. She got why Vicki had been clawing at the ground. At a ninety-degree angle from the rhododendron, there was the pine cone Noah had found buried in the dirt. Using a piece of the bark as a shovel, Lou moved the surrounding dirt, hoping to unearth it and whatever was below.

The pine cone popped out of the ground, and underneath, in a small hole that had been dug into the earth, was a key. Lou held it up, her eyes sparkling as she and Noah took it all in.

"What do you think you're doing?" a deep voice cut through their surprise, making them both jump. James stood a few feet behind them, his arms crossed and his expression dark. "Lou? Why are you digging around in the bank's landscaping?"

She blinked to get her bearings. "What are you doing here?" she asked. "I thought the bank was closed."

"I was just finishing up some paperwork," James said, adding, "not that it's any of your business."

"We found something," Lou said quickly, noticing that James's patience was rapidly deteriorating, and she needed him on their side. "I think Vicki might've hidden it here."

James stepped forward. "That's a safe-deposit box key."

The three of them shared an excited glance before rushing inside the bank. James used a very full key ring to open the bank door, locking it behind them. Lou noticed Tiffany was still working as well. Of course, the two lived together, and their new house was a twenty-minute drive south. They probably drove together each day, and she had to wait for him.

At the sight of James, Tiffany perked up from where she'd been counting money into a till. "What are you doing, honey?" she asked as he led Lou and Noah into the side room where the safe-deposit boxes were.

"Uh, we found a safe-deposit key buried outside. We're just checking it," James explained to Tiffany as she joined them. "We shouldn't get our hopes up. I would've known if Vicki had started a safe-deposit box, and I can say with certainty that she didn't."

"Who didn't?" Tiffany asked, surprising everyone now that she stood behind them.

"Vicki Younger, the woman who was selling stocks in her serum company," James said. "The one who was killed last week."

Tiffany placed a hand over her heart. "She was *killed*?" Her mouth parted.

"You didn't hear?" Lou asked, hiding the better part of the incredulity she felt. Where had she been?

Tiffany shook her head. "We're doing a bathroom remodel right now, and Jamesey and I have been so busy. I didn't realize. Vicki had a safe-deposit box. I should know. I opened it for her."

James stared at her in surprise. "What? Why didn't you tell me?"

"I didn't know it was important." Tiffany sighed in exasperation.

James rushed through the safe-deposit room door and peered at the key, checking the number engraved on the side. He found the matching box and used the dirty key to open it. Pulling out the box and placing it on the counter, James waited a beat as if allowing them all to catch their breath before he opened it.

Inside, stacks of money lined the box. There had to be thousands, tens of thousands, if Lou had to guess.

Noah stepped forward. "We need to get Roy over here now."

CHAPTER 19

Roy exhaled as he took in the sheer amount of cash sitting in the safe-deposit box on the counter.

"And here I thought this week couldn't get any weirder," he said.

Lou wondered if he'd gotten a moment's rest that entire week. She also wondered if Officer Little had found any more bugs in the coffee shop. She thought about texting George to ask, but realized she'd left her phone in her purse in Noah's truck.

"This is even more than she collected in Button and Brine combined," Roy said as he scanned the pile of money.

"She must've been saving it for a while, hiding it from Todd." Lou rocked back on her heels.

"Which would be yet another motive for Todd to kill her if—" Noah began.

"Todd hadn't also been strangled in the same way Vicki was," Lou finished for him.

"Which suggests that it was someone who was after both of them," Roy added. "We're looking into other places they might've hit. I think we might have a lead with a pair of towns down by the Oregon and Washington border. They didn't change their names, which surprised me, but their descriptions came back similar. Apparently, they like to find two small towns who hate each other and aren't likely to share information. They play them off one another, knowing they can gain trust easily by badmouthing the other town." Roy blinked. "Lou, didn't you tell me that Todd mentioned being followed?"

"By a beekeeper," Lou said, repeating the information she'd given him yesterday. She still had no idea what it meant, but Silas had been right about Vicki having been searching for something around the bank, so it seemed plausible that the rest of his information was correct as well.

"Thank you." Roy dipped his chin toward Lou and Noah. "You two are free to go. We'll let you know if we have questions."

They turned to leave. Just as they exited the bank into the muggy evening air, Lou's stomach grumbled. It was then that she remembered she and Noah had been on their way to eat when they'd figured out that Vicki might've been hiding something around the bank. She glanced over at Noah, and she was about to ask where he wanted to eat, when she remembered the very last part of Silas's account of Vicki's movements during the last hour of her life.

"What are you squinting at?" Noah asked, trying to follow her gaze toward the houses next to the bank on Hem Avenue.

"Everything else Silas said has turned out to be true," Lou said. "They *were* being followed by someone wearing a beekeeping costume. Vicki *was* digging around and kicking at the bricks of the bank building. Who's to say she didn't actually disappear in the alley between those two houses?" Lou motioned to the house that stood next to the bank and the one behind it.

Without overthinking, Lou walked forward until she could see the space between the two houses. It was a concrete strip about two cars in length. A tall fence sat at the end of the driveway, cutting it off from the same forest that sat behind the bank. It looked like an alley between businesses, only it was sandwiched between two houses instead, and Silas was right, with the fence running along the back, there was no way out.

Noah, who'd followed Lou, walked forward. He stopped as he looked at the space in between the white and blue houses. There weren't any low windows or doors on the sides of the houses, so she couldn't have slipped inside either of them via the alley. "There really isn't anywhere for her to go." Noah observed. "Unless she could vault over a six-foot fence."

Vicki had been a short woman. There was no way she could've scaled that in the seconds it took for Silas to follow her and round the corner. "What if there's a hidden door in the fence?" Lou walked forward, inspecting the wooden slats. "The forest where I found her is right behind this, so it would make sense that she escaped through here and went back to her car."

Noah helped Lou search, pushing on boards, analyzing the tiniest details that might signify a moveable panel or hidden hinge.

"It would have to be something that opens and closes

easily if she slipped through before Silas could catch her," Noah said, thinking aloud.

Lou's gaze moved from the fence to the side of the white house to her right. There was a vertical cut in the horizontal wood siding. She followed it up, noting that it took a sharp turn to the right, outlining a door shape. She could only see it because she was standing straight on, so they hadn't noticed it from the street or the beginning of the alley.

"Like this?" Lou asked, taking a guess and pushing in on the side of the house.

It took Lou shoving her body weight into the door, but it finally swung inward.

Noah jogged over, stepping forward into the dark basement while Lou was still holding the door open. "I wonder where this goes," he whispered as he ducked his head and went farther in. "It looks like it's a dead end, just a storage space."

Lou wanted to check it out for herself. She tried to carefully close the door, but the weight of it threw her off-balance, ripping the thing from her fingers and closing behind her, blanketing them in darkness.

"Noah?" she whispered, her voice shaking with the adrenaline of the moment.

"Here." His voice felt close and far away all at once.

There wasn't a shred of light in the place.

"How many steps did you take inside?" Lou asked, reaching forward, not wanting to trip on something. She'd been so focused on the door itself that she hadn't used the time while it was open to look into the space.

"Just a few." He kept his voice low, especially with how

deep it was. "Sorry, I forgot you don't have your phone," he said with a chuckle.

She waited for him to turn on his flashlight, but all she saw was a quick flash of a screen before a muted clatter sounded on the concrete.

"Um … did you see where that fell?" Noah whispered, an edge of panic to his tone.

Lou blinked into the darkness. "I didn't." The light of his phone screen felt burned into her retina, but without any bearings, she felt directionless. Still, she took a shaky step into the basement toward his voice, swiping at the darkness with her hands. The feeling was wholly unsettling. "I'm heading toward you, I think," she said.

This time, when he spoke, his voice was lower. "I'm just trying to feel around for it," he said with a grunt as he seemed to be reaching around where he was standing. "Here. I'll stand so you can find me."

Lou took another step forward, but still couldn't find Noah. She was about to call out for him again, needing his voice as an anchor, when her fingers brushed against soft cotton. Acting on instinct instead of rational thought, Lou patted the object, testing it out. Her fingers swept over burly arms and a muscled back. Fingertips gripping his T-shirt, Lou pulled herself forward until she was next to him.

He turned around, wrapping his arms around her. "I've got you," he whispered, holding her to him.

"Whose house is this?" she asked, her body immediately relaxing now that she was with Noah again.

"Allen Kettle," he answered.

"The editor of the *Button Post*?"

"Yeah," he said, the word barely a breath.

Footsteps sounded above them. A chair creaked as a person seemed to sit down in it.

"Should we call for help?" Lou asked, noticing that they both froze at the reminder that someone was above them instead of calling out.

Noah stiffened, whispering, "It doesn't bother you that Vicki obviously came here before she died?"

Lou took a beat to answer. She'd been so focused on the darkness and trying to find Noah's phone that she'd totally let that slip her mind. "You think he could've hurt her? What reason would he have?"

Noah's shoulders lifted, then released. "She was trespassing?"

About to argue that wasn't a good enough reason to justify killing someone, Lou froze as she heard a sound come through the vent above their heads. It was a conversation, but it sounded like women, not anyone named Allen. She would've assumed he just had company over, but the voices began to sound increasingly familiar, as did the conversation.

"Is that … me?" she whispered with a gasp. "It is. And George."

The sound of chattering filled the background and a coffee steamer screamed in the distance.

Lou's mind clicked the pieces together. "The coffee shop bug. Allen must be the *BSB*."

On the recording, George gasped and asked, "Did something happen between you and Noah?"

A chill wound down Lou's spine as she recognized exactly what she was hearing. The conversation she had with George in the coffee shop the other day—the one she'd been worried the *BSB* would write a post about.

There was nothing she could do to stop it. After a beat, the recorded version of her said the familiar words.

"I mean, nothing's happened yet, but I think I want something to, and it's freaking me out. I'm not sure how to go from being friends to more but it seems like lately we're always just a few inches from kissing."

Lou's fingers gripped Noah's shirt tighter as she listened, her recorded words coming back as if they were in the same room as Allen. She had the urge to reach up and cover Noah's ears, but probably couldn't have found them in the darkness in time, anyway.

Mercifully, the clip stopped with a click of a computer mouse. The sound of keyboard keys clacking sounded after that. It sounded like he was writing up one heck of a blog post about her and Noah.

The strong wall holding her up shifted, reminding her it was a person. Embarrassment surged through her all over again, like a second electric shock. As if the first one hadn't done enough damage.

"Noah, I..." She didn't know how to finish that sentence, however.

It turned out she didn't need to.

"Did you mean that?" His voice was soft, his tone wary.

She closed her eyes. It didn't make a difference with the lack of light, but it gave her the strength to whisper, "Yes." She cringed, waiting for his reaction.

Noah's hands found her face. He gently tilted her chin up, causing her eyes to close again when his lips met hers. She took a step closer, wrapping her arms around him as he deepened the kiss. Her whole body tingled, and she reached up to place a hand on his cheek just as he pulled back, breathing hard.

"I'm sorry," he rasped out the apology.

"Why?" she asked, smoothing her thumb along his beard-covered jawline.

He chuckled. "I don't know. I just … lost control there. Something about the darkness."

Lou felt it too. As much as she'd wanted to kiss Noah over the past week—or more—they were friends. That was a hard hurdle to get over. But in the dark of Allen's basement, it felt like they were just two souls, existing in the space, removed from their pasts and their presents.

Words formed in Lou's mind. Responses that might ease his worries came to her in droves. But she shoved them all back as she brought her other hand to his face and leaned up, starting the kiss this time. She hoped that would be enough to show him that he had nothing to be sorry for.

He let his arms drop, like he might be dumbstruck, but he quickly wrapped his arms around her back and pulled her close to him, as close as she could get. She could feel him breathe her in. When she finally pulled away, he rested his forehead against hers.

"You have no idea how long I've wanted to do that." His voice was as rough as his beard had been against her face.

Lou's whole body was tingling with happiness. "I think I might have an idea," she answered, her own voice sounding almost as hoarse. Reality came crashing back down on her like a cold wave. She pulled back. "Wait. I thought you weren't ready to move on."

"Why would you think that?"

She wet her lips. "The other day, on your porch, you said you were finally feeling ready a while back but then you had to remind yourself to be patient."

Noah's hand settled gently on her cheek. Because of the darkness, it made her jump slightly at first. "I meant that I was waiting for you," he said. "I've been ready since the day I met you, Lou."

"Oh." She almost laughed at her misunderstanding.

"You've been through so much. I didn't want to rush you."

"Thank you." Through all her happiness, Lou remembered where they were and the situation they were in. Finding Noah's hand in the darkness, Lou said, "Well, we stumbled on to the identity of the *BSB*. What do you think our odds are of getting out of this basement in one piece so we can tell Roy?"

"I'm going to spin you around. We can walk in the direction we came from together." Noah leaned down, so he spoke directly into her ear, "Once we open the door, we can look for my phone."

As they moved through the space, the keyboard clacking above stopped. Freezing to listen, worried they'd been found out, they settled once another round of recordings started. This time, it wasn't Lou speaking, but it was Martie complaining that her van's tires needed to be rotated, but she couldn't find the time with all the work she was getting, surrounding the convention.

Allen had moved on to another story.

They continued to feel for the door. There were boxes, things that felt like gardening tools, and old furniture. Lou's fingers curled each time she touched something she didn't expect, her mind playing evil pictures of her sticking her hand into a spider's web or cutting her fingers on old broken glass. Noah's arm reached around her, feeling as well.

That was when the typing above stopped again and something else started. Allen tapped his feet in a rhythm as he paused, as if he were thinking. His feet drummed in a staccato beat that sounded a lot like the "Happy Birthday" song.

Lou's whole body shuddered. She'd heard that before. So had Noah. It had been the odd video that had been on Vicki's phone, the one Roy had shared with them at the very beginning of the case. But why had Vicki been recording Allen in the dark of the basement?

Suddenly, Lou could think of an overwhelming reason for Allen to want Vicki dead. If she'd snuck into his house and recorded him listening to town gossip and found out he was the *BSB*, he might've strangled her to keep her quiet.

"We need to get out of here," Lou whispered, her movements becoming more frantic.

CHAPTER 20

In the seemingly endless dark of Allen Kettle's basement, Lou's fingers finally closed around a handle. She pulled with all her strength, wrenching the hidden door toward them and letting them spill out of the space. They blinked in the blindingly bright sunlight as they spilled out into the alley. Lou held the door open as Noah went back in, retrieving his phone from the floor, tucked halfway under a small side table.

Once he had that, they ran until they reached the bank. Gasping to catch her breath, Lou placed a hand on each of her knees as she bent forward. Noah panted next to her, laying a hand on her back as he looked behind them, like he expected Allen to chase after them, when in reality, he probably hadn't even realized they were in his basement.

"What are you two doing?" The voice made them both jump, and Lou screamed.

Turning, they found Roy leaving the bank. Even though it had felt like forever, they must not have been in the basement for all that long.

"You look like you're running from a serial killer." Roy smirked, but the expression fell as he seemed to remember that he was investigating not just one, but two murders at that very moment.

Lou hooked a thumb back toward Allen's house. "The recording. Vicki's phone. The one with the people talking. And the 'Happy Birthday' rhythm. It was Allen." She panted in between each short sentence.

"Seriously?" Roy blinked, as if his mind was catching up with him. He reached for his phone and put in a call. "I need backup at—" He held the phone away from his mouth as he looked at Noah.

"Twenty-three Hem Avenue," Noah supplied.

Roy repeated it, then said, "Yes, a suspect in the Vicki Younger murder, possibly in the Todd Meadows murder as well."

While they waited, Lou and Noah explained to Roy all about the secret entrance they'd found into Allen's basement and what they'd heard while in there.

Rushing off when his backup arrived, Lou and Noah were left by themselves, standing outside of the bank. Noah raked a hand through his hair. Lou swallowed, memories of their kiss flooding back to her now that they were out of danger once more. Noah's eyes locked on to hers, and they were just crinkling up into the beginnings of a smile when his phone began to ring.

He glanced down. "Sorry, it's Cricket." Swiping at the screen, he asked, "Hey, what's up?" His eyebrows furrowed as he listened.

Lou couldn't hear the exact words Cricket was saying,

but from the volume and speed with which they spilled through the speaker, she could guess it wasn't good.

"Are you serious? I'll be right there." He ended the call, jaw clenching. "They just closed the convention for the evening and the sponsors told my mom this is going to be their last year. They're pulling their support."

"Why?" Lou asked, but as soon as the question was out, she knew the answer. "The second murder?" she asked with a cringe.

"I think so. They said this town is too problematic for them, and they'd like to take the convention somewhere a little more wholesome." Noah grimaced. "I'm so sorry. I've got to go talk to my parents and see if I can help."

Lou waved him away. "Of course. Maybe you can talk to the sponsors yourself, hint that the killer's in custody? That might help soothe their worries." She knew he couldn't say anything concrete about the arrest, but knowing there had been one had to make the sponsors feel better.

After getting her purse from his truck, Noah drove off toward the park. Lou walked home as the sun began to set. She hated to call Willow and bug her, but she'd also just kissed Noah and needed to tell someone. Hurrying home, she fed the cats, and settled on the couch before dialing her friend's number.

"Hey," Willow answered. The sound of bubbling water was loud in the background. "Sorry, I'm in the hot tub. Can you hear me?"

"Only barely," Lou said.

"Uh..." There was a pause on Willow's end, and the

bubbling ceased in the background. "Say something now. I turned off the jets."

"I kissed Noah." Lou let the statement hang there as if it were an ornament on a tree that she was admiring.

Willow groaned. "Sorry, I think it's still too loud with the river rushing in the background. All I heard was something about you kissing Noah."

"You heard right, Willow. I kissed him. He kissed me. We kissed each other." Lou's face flared with heat as she replayed the wonderful moment in her mind.

Willow let out a surprised laugh. "Wait. You did? That's amazing." She cleared her throat. "It was, right?" There was a hint of worry hanging in her tone.

"Yes, more than amazing," Lou said. "You know, if you get past the crippling guilt I'm experiencing after kissing someone other than Ben, and that we caught a killer right after the fact, sure. It's great."

"Vicki's killer?" Willow asked. "Hold on. I've got to get to a quieter place." There was a muffled noise, as if Willow had placed her hand over the receiver. "Easton, I'm going inside for a minute to talk to Lou." After a moment of water dripping and feet padding, as she must've grabbed a towel to wrap herself in, Willow said, "Okay, I'm in the kitchen, and it's quiet. What's going on over there?"

Lou filled her in on all of it, on how Todd had been Vicki's accomplice, how he'd been killed by the same strangler, how she and Noah had found the money Vicki had stashed away, and how they'd stumbled upon the basement where she'd "disappeared" when Silas had been chasing after her.

"Allen Kettle?" Willow asked. "The editor of the newspaper?"

"Yup." Lou bobbed her head. "When she was hiding in his basement, she must've overheard him listening to the recordings from the coffee shop and tried to blackmail him."

But as Lou recounted it to her best friend, it didn't feel quite right anymore. Whereas earlier, when they'd been telling Roy, it had seemed like the obvious conclusion, but now it felt flat. Allen hadn't heard Noah and Lou in the basement. What was to say he'd caught Vicki? Also, if she *had* blackmailed him, why wouldn't he have taken her phone or at least erased the incriminating video of him? Hadn't Roy said he'd found her phone sitting next to her in the car?

Lou's gut sank as she realized Roy quite possibly had the wrong person in custody.

"Lou," Willow said sternly, her tone telling Lou that hadn't been the first time she'd said her name. "You still there?"

"Yeah. Sorry." She shook her head. "I think I just realized it couldn't have been Allen."

"He's not the *BSB*?" Willow asked.

"No. I mean, yes, he's still the *BSB*, but I'm starting to doubt that he killed Vicki or Todd," Lou said.

"Okay…" Frustration bit through Willow's tone. "Are you going to tell me more about you and Noah, or are you trying to torture me?" She chuckled.

"Oh, sorry. My mind is all over the place. It was … amazing, Willow." Lou couldn't help the grin that spread over her face. "He overheard a recording the *BSB* had of me telling George about my feelings for him, and we were in the dark in the basement, and it was like the darkness was the cloak we needed to get over our fears."

Willow let out a long "Awww."

"And it was so romantic. Like, romance book material." Lou sank back into the couch cushions.

"What does it mean? Did you have time to talk to him about it?" Willow asked.

Lou frowned. "Noah got called away to help his family with an issue with the convention, so we didn't get a chance to debrief, but I'm sure we will." At least, she hoped they would. The thought wobbled through her with uncertainty.

Willow seemed to hold none of the doubt. "Well, I want to hear all about it when I come home tomorrow." She sighed. "As much as I'll be sad to leave this place, I'm missing home."

"Home's missing you a *ton*," Lou told her. "Things don't feel right here without you. I hope you and Easton have a good last day."

"I will. And you make sure to have a conversation with Noah," she teased before hanging up.

Lou tapped her fingernails against her phone case while she thought, letting herself get lost in the memory of her and Noah for a moment. Jolting back to reality, she remembered she needed to send the text to Roy.

Hey, sorry to throw a wrench into things, but I'm wondering if Allen could be innocent. 1. He didn't get rid of her phone or the incriminating video. 2. Why would he have killed Todd?

She only had to wait a few moments before Roy texted back.

> Yeah … we realized the same thing about ten minutes into questioning him. I still think he's lying about something, but not the murder. We let him go a few minutes ago. He's going to come clean about the BSB stuff, and he told us where more of the bugs were hidden in the ice cream shop, the bakery, and the park, but other than that, I think we're still on the hunt for the real killer.

Lou sighed, frustrated but happy that her gut hadn't been wrong. She sent a quick response.

> Okay. Let me know if there's anything I can do.

> Thanks. I will.

Lou should've felt better. Even though they didn't have a killer, that matter was settled for now. But her stomach still felt like it was on one of those Tilt-A-Whirl rides at the fair. Her lungs felt tight with anxious energy, and her knee bounced up and down as she tapped her foot in rhythm to her rapid heartbeat.

It was Noah. She knew she couldn't kiss that man just the one time. And it was killing her not to know what he was thinking. While she knew he'd left to help his family, she had been hoping he might text or call after that was finished.

As soon as the worry filled her, she relaxed. If the last

year and a half had taught her anything, it was that she could trust that man. If he had the time to come over or text, he would've. The fact that he hadn't meant he was still dealing with the quilt convention drama with his family.

The knowledge that she trusted Noah didn't make Lou any less fidgety. And while she was normally content to spend her evenings on the couch with a book and the cats, she had a feeling it wouldn't cut it tonight.

As if to remind her of her options, Catticus chose that moment to stroll through the room. He didn't have a hint of his limp anymore, proving he was as quick to heal as he was to put himself in danger. Lou smirked and pulled out her phone. She texted Sebastian.

> Catticus seems to be all healed. Do you have time for me to stop by with him tomorrow after I close the bookshop? Or … I'm not busy tonight, if it's not too late.

Lou didn't know what she expected—possibly that a millionaire such as Sebastian would be too busy doing important millionaire things to get back to her right away— but a response came through within a minute.

> I'm here. Bring him on by. I'll watch for you at the gate.

It looked like she had something to occupy her evening after all. She got to work packing up Catticus to go to his new home, and then she and the feline headed to the mansion on the hill.

CHAPTER 21

Sebastian Andrade's modern mansion on the hill was the inviting sight Lou needed after a long day. The large windows and modern, angular design of the house made it so it practically glowed as the sun dipped below the mountains. Warm light radiated out from the place, making it look like a beacon as Lou drove up and parked in the circular driveway.

She got Catticus Finch's crate from the back seat—the same one Sebastian had loaned her to bring Meatball to her house—and approached the entryway. This time, it wasn't Sebastian who met her at the expansive front steps, but a woman whom she immediately assumed to be Lisa, his cook, based on the apron she wore.

"He's just inside. Come in," Lisa told Lou, gesturing for her to follow.

The crate rocked to one side as Catticus moved to the front, sniffing the air of his new home. He let out a low meow as the front door closed behind them. Lou's heart tightened with worry. What if he didn't like it here? She talked herself through the anxiety, reminding her worried mind that she could always bring him back to the bookshop. He didn't have to stay here just because she'd taken Meatball.

Sebastian walked in from the kitchen. He wore khaki shorts and a regular cotton T-shirt, looking just like anyone else in Button.

"There he is." He knelt in front of the crate, and Lou set it on the floor. "Catticus Finch," Sebastian said, chuckling. "Too clever."

Lou grinned. "Are any of your cats territorial, or do you think we can just let him out?" She really wanted to see how Catticus did in the house before leaving him.

Sebastian didn't even wait. He opened the crate door and swung it open. "They're all very chill. We have a lot of cats coming and going because of all the rescuing I do."

Catticus sniffed the hand Sebastian held forward, rubbing his face against it before striding out of the crate. Lou had, at that point in her fostering journey, seen many cats exit crates into a new space. Some cowered in the back of the crate, refusing to come out. Others raced out in search of a new hiding place. The most popular way out was to slink warily until they got their bearings. Catticus was the first cat she'd seen walk out as if he already owned the place.

"Of course he's already comfortable." Lou chuckled.

Catticus's gaze locked on to one of the cat towers standing next to the large windows. He raced over to it, vaulting up the levels until he stood at the very top. Then he followed a small ramp up along the wall to an even higher perch.

"You were right. He's just the cat to appreciate a climbing course like this." Sebastian watched Catticus flop onto his side and clean his paws on the ledge.

Lou exhaled the breath she'd been holding, any bits of worry that he might not adapt finally letting go. "I'm so glad. I thought he would, but you never know with cats."

"They're particular creatures." Sebastian's eyes lit up.

"Of course, if he ever seems off, you're free to call me," Lou said. "I'll come take him back." She knelt and closed the crate door.

Sebastian eyed Lou. "Do you have somewhere to be, or would you like to stay for dinner?"

The mention of food reminded Lou she and Noah had never made it to dinner. "I can stay," she said with a shrug. The view of the sunset sweeping over the valley from the living room was gorgeous as well, and she wouldn't mind the company.

He beamed, then walked over to the kitchen where Lisa was cleaning up after dinner and stooped to peer into a wine fridge.

"Does white wine sound okay?" he asked. "Lisa made amazing pasta with local mushrooms, and I think this will pair nicely with her culinary masterpiece." He held up a chilled bottle of white.

Lisa's cheeks went red with embarrassment. She tutted and shook her head. "He's too nice."

"I don't think so," Lou said. "I had some of your sushi the other day, and it was delicious."

Lisa smiled. "I'm so glad."

As Sebastian plated their food, letting Lisa focus on the clean up, Lou stood. She searched for an enormous table like she'd seen at Francis's mansion. But Sebastian brought the bowl over to the couch.

"Stay put. You can eat where you are." He handed over a bowl of pasta and set a glass of white wine next to her, then went back to grab his own glass. "So, how's the case going?" he asked once he was seated in the love seat next to the couch.

"Not great. We thought we had the killer earlier, but I think we got it wrong." Lou took her first bite, eyes widening as the nutty flavor of the mushrooms and the cream sauce Lisa had used met her taste buds. "Lisa, this is amazing."

"I'm glad you like it," Lisa called from the kitchen.

"What made you think this person was the killer?" Sebastian asked, focusing on the case rather than the meal.

Lou explained how they'd found the basement where Vicki must've hidden and how she'd had a recording of Allen on her phone.

"Ah, so he's the *BSB*," Sebastian said. "But Allen wouldn't have any reason to kill Vicki, and definitely not Todd. He didn't invest in their fake company."

Lou nodded. "That's what we realized later. Plus, if he'd known about the video she had, proving he was the *BSB*, why wouldn't he have erased it or taken her phone?"

"So you're back to square one," Sebastian said, pursing his lips as he thought. He took a sip of his wine. "My PI hasn't come back with anything new, either, so I'm no help."

Lou swallowed a bite and washed it down with a sip of her wine. "Has he said anything about a beekeeper's suit?" Lou asked, not letting on that she'd met Wesley. She didn't want to embarrass the young man by divulging to his employer that he'd come to her for help.

Sebastian narrowed his eyes. "Not at all. Why?"

Lou explained the things Silas had seen before Vicki died, and how Todd had commented on the person in the suit following them around before he'd also been killed. "Even though it sounded like rambling at first, everything Silas saw has turned out to be important in this case. I just don't want to count out the beekeeper suit, since that's the only thing that we still can't explain."

"Smart." Sebastian sipped his wine, his attention drifting off to the other side of the room as he seemed to ponder that. "Now that you mention it, I think Wesley did say something about seeing a person drive around in a bright green car with a full beekeeper suit on. He said he thought that old man was crazy when he mentioned it at first, but then he saw it too. He just wasn't sure how it was connected to the case."

"That makes two of us," Lou said incredulously as she swallowed the last bite of her dish. "Thank you. That was just what I needed."

Sebastian stood to grab her empty bowl, taking it over to the kitchen and placing it in the dishwasher himself, even though Lisa was already working on the dishes. Lou really liked how he seemed to do a lot more for himself than Francis. Not that she blamed Francis. If she had a butler who would do almost everything for her, she couldn't say that she wouldn't take advantage of that. But Sebastian seemed a lot more approachable and relatable because he did so much on his own.

"How'd you get into the cat rescuing?" Lou asked once

Sebastian rejoined her in the living room. She sat back with her glass of wine now that her stomach was full and happy.

Sebastian laughed. "It's actually a funny story. I was driving down a more remote road in the valley one day, and I saw a kitten in the street. I stopped my car, got out, and picked it up. The moment I had it in my hands, about ten of its brothers and sisters scampered out of the tall grass along the side of the road. I took them all home, slowly finding houses for each one, except Cheese." He gestured to a long-haired orange cat stretched out along the back of the couch. "He's got a heart condition that requires him to be on medication, and I knew his medical bills would be too high for just anyone, so I kept him."

Lou tilted her head. "That's lovely of you."

He shrugged off her compliment as if it wasn't a big deal. "The next time I drove down that road, I found Fig." He motioned to a white cat curled in a hammock on the wall behind Lou. "She was older, but just like the kittens, it was clear that they'd been around humans before and had been dumped in that field."

"How awful." Lou couldn't understand people who mistreated animals. Dumping pets they didn't want in a field was a cowardly decision. "I'm glad you found her."

"I started checking the place every few days. It's like these people talk to each other and they decide, oh, let's all use this same field to dump the pets we thought we wanted, but now don't." His grip was tightening around the fragile stem of his wineglass. "From there, cats in need just seem to find me."

Lou admired the space. "You've made this a feline paradise."

He beamed. "You should see the bedroom." His cheeks reddened, and he held up a hand. "Not like that. Sorry." He let out an awkward laugh. "I just mean, there are even more beds and obstacles in there. I also had a custom frame made that has a whole kitty maze underneath, so they can run around in there when they inevitably get their middle-of-the-night spurts of energy."

"I know those zoomies well." Lou laughed. "Catticus will appreciate the maze, I'm sure."

Sapphire wasn't so bad anymore, but Catnip Everdeen liked to get in the shower where sounds echoed and meow like a small tiger sometimes.

"Lou, I—" Sebastian cut off, rubbing at the back of his neck. His face was still red from his earlier comment, and he couldn't seem to meet her eyes. "I don't suppose you'd be interested in having dinner with me sometime."

Lou couldn't help but glance over at the kitchen where he'd so recently put her used bowl.

"I know we just *had* dinner," he said. "I mean, like a date."

Swallowing, Lou met Sebastian's gaze. "That's very kind, Sebastian. I think all I can offer right now is friendship, though."

"Right." He shook his head. "Because of your late husband. I should've known."

And as much as Lou knew she didn't owe him an explanation, she liked Sebastian as a person and felt he deserved the truth.

"Actually, I have feelings for someone else," she said, loving how it felt to say it aloud.

It didn't matter to her that she didn't know where Noah

stood after their kiss. She would've said no to Sebastian regardless. Because the truth was, she'd known Noah was the right person for her to move on with for a long time, and no matter how long it took for him to feel ready for a relationship, she wanted to wait.

"I appreciate your candidness." Squinting one eye, Sebastian asked, "Is it the vet I met the other day?"

Lou couldn't help but grin like a teenager in love. "It is."

"I thought I caught something between the two of you." Sebastian sighed. "Well, I wish you the best of luck. He'd be a fool to let you pass by. *But* if he does, promise me you'll give my offer a second chance."

She could do that.

But Noah was no fool, and Lou knew—especially after that kiss—that she wouldn't be able to move on to anyone else. She hoped the same was true for him.

CHAPTER 22

When Lou pulled her car into the alley behind Whiskers and Words a short while later, she was still smiling. Hanging out with Sebastian had been fun. They'd spent a little more time playing with Catticus Finch to make sure he was feeling settled before going home.

But as Lou slammed her car door shut and pulled out her keys to open the back door of the bookshop, her heart jumped into her throat. Out of the shadows stepped a man, cloaked in the alley's darkness. He'd hidden away in the area just beyond her security cameras, so he wouldn't set them off and alert her to his presence.

Any momentary fear washed away in the moment that followed her jump, however. The man had known where the camera's blind spots were because he'd installed them.

"Noah?" she asked, even though there was no doubt it was him from the way her heart felt warm in his presence.

"I didn't mean to scare you." He stepped forward into

the light spilling down the alley from the streetlights. "I just ... I didn't want to wait at the front door."

Lou swallowed, understanding. As complicated as her situation was—because grief was not only tricky to navigate but something that would be with her for the rest of her life—Noah lived in the same town as his ex-wife, and his daughter had already proven that the children of Button were just as well-informed as the adults.

"It's not that I don't want people to know—" He stopped as if he wasn't sure how to finish that thought.

She didn't take offense at his reasoning at all. "But it's new, and you have Marigold." Grimacing, Lou remembered something. "I may have spilled the secret to Willow and Easton. I'm so sorry."

Noah shook his head. "Oh, them? I don't mind that. It'll be nice to have someone who knows. I trust them to keep our secret."

"Okay, good." Lou laughed. "I'm glad I didn't ruin everything." She tucked her hands into her pockets. "Do you want to come up?"

"Desperately." His voice was rough, just like it had been in the darkness of Allen's basement.

A shiver of happiness trickled over Lou's skin, and she unlocked the back door. "I just dropped Catticus off at his new home. He was in heaven."

"I think that'll be a great place for him," Noah said as he followed her inside. "I'm sorry it took me so long to get here. My family's in crisis mode. The sponsors are officially done. It took a few hours, but they finally decided that maybe it's best if we don't continue the convention. Just the thought of finding new sponsors practically had my mom in hives."

Lou stopped in the middle of the staircase and turned back to Noah. "I'm so sorry. That's terrible. I know how much it's meant to your family, not to mention the whole town." Like so many other moments, Lou felt the urge to wrap her arms around him. Unlike every other time, she gave in to the feeling.

The fact that she was a step in front of him meant they were at eye level. Noah leaned into her embrace and then pulled her into another kiss. Her lips peeled into a smile before the kiss was over. Noah's did too. He pulled back, his eyes sparkling in the dimly lit stairway.

"What?" he asked even though, based on the look he was giving her, he understood *exactly* what she was feeling.

Leaning into him, she said, "I'm just happy."

"You're sure you don't mind keeping things under wraps for a bit?" he asked. "I just want to see how we do as more than friends first, before I bring Marigold into this. Mostly because I think she's going to be so thrilled that I wouldn't want us to break her heart if it didn't work out."

She loved his concern for his daughter. Marigold had already gone through one breakup between her parents. If they could spare the girl unnecessary heartache and worry, Lou was all for it.

"I don't mind at all," she said. "In fact, sneaking around like this is kind of fun."

He smiled. "It still doesn't feel real. I think I might be dreaming."

Taking his hand, she led him the rest of the way up the stairs to her apartment. Noah settled onto the couch, petting Sapphire where he lay curled up on a blanket Lou had draped over the back. Lou sat next to him, tucking her feet underneath her.

"What do you think your family will do now?" Lou asked.

Noah raked a hand down his face. "They have to figure out how to tell the town. After last year, everyone realized how much the businesses depend on the income from the tourists."

Lou nodded. "Your parents can't blame themselves, though. And Roy's doing his best to figure out who the killer is, though I doubt it's anyone in town."

At that, Noah's eyebrows jumped up. "Wait. Isn't it Allen?"

That was right. He hadn't heard.

She told him about the doubts that had cropped up after she'd talked to Willow. "Apparently, Roy found the same to be true as he questioned him, and they let him go with a warning about the recordings."

Noah didn't need much convincing. "That makes sense now that I think of it." Still, it took him a beat to catch up before he said, "And you're pretty sure it's no one in town?"

"Pretty sure is being generous." She chuckled. "I just can't help but go back to the beekeeper's suit."

Noah frowned. "The one Silas saw the day Vicki died?"

"And that Todd cited as evidence he was being followed. I think I've seen it around town too. Glimpses, at least." Lou scratched Meatball behind the ears as she jumped onto the couch, searching for a lap to occupy.

"But no one in town keeps bees, do they?" Noah asked, trying to find the connection.

Lou tipped her head to one side. "That's a good point. I didn't check local apiarists, but something about Todd saying they were being followed got me thinking it had to be someone from a past scam."

"Roy said that he had a lead in the last place they ran their pyramid scheme." As if Meatball's contented purrs had let out a call that there were laps available, Anne Mice came out from the bedroom and settled on Noah. "What does he think about the beekeeper suit?"

Lou scoffed. Roy may have been doing a lot better at listening to her this time around, but he was still a dubious man, and she could tell the beekeeping suit still hadn't made it onto his list of clues to take seriously.

"I doubt he thinks it's connected in any way," Lou said.

Noah sighed. "If only Todd hadn't run away from you so quickly. It sounded like he knew who it was, at least."

Lou gasped, pulling in a quick breath. "Omigosh, Noah. That's it."

He blinked. "What?"

"The video Roy let us listen to on Vicki's phone. There was a man and a woman talking. Vicki wouldn't necessarily care about any two Buttonites talking. But what if it was her and Todd, and that's why she recorded it?" Lou suggested.

"But the *BSB* never wrote anything about Vicki or Todd besides that initial post about the serum," Noah said, confusion dragging out each word.

Lou moved the cat off her lap and stood. "Exactly. So Roy was right. He said he thought Allen was still lying about something, but it wasn't about the murder. I think Vicki blackmailed him into keeping her connection to Todd a secret."

Noah's eyes flashed with intrigue. "We have to go ask him about it."

Lou grabbed her purse. "Just what I was thinking. I'll drive."

They scampered down the stairs and to Lou's car. She drove through the dark streets of Button probably too fast but felt as if they were already one step behind, and any extra seconds could mean the difference between finding the answers they sought and coming up empty-handed. She pulled into the alley between Allen's house and his neighbor's.

Noah's phone pinged. "Roy's on his way, with backup. Now we wait, I guess," Noah said, tapping his fingers on his thighs in a rhythm that sounded just like Lou's nervous heartbeat.

"Or … we could go talk to him before Roy gets here," Lou suggested. "You know how people are around cops sometimes."

"And he's already lied to Roy, so he might be more likely to admit that he lied to us than to someone who could arrest him for obstructing justice." Noah nodded.

That settled, they climbed out of Lou's car and headed to Allen's home. The lights were on inside, so that was a good sign. Noah knocked a second time when Allen didn't come to the door after a few moments. Then the door swung open, and Allen stood on the other side. He looked flushed and nervous.

Lou's gaze flicked over to Noah's, and she narrowed her eyes almost imperceptibly, hoping he got the hint that she was going to take the lead and he should follow along.

"Allen, we know you lied." She barged into his house, not even asking to be invited. She channeled all the New York City energy she'd built up over the past couple of decades.

Noah followed her.

"I-uh-what? How?" Allen's entire face was flushed now, and his fingers practically shook as he closed the door behind them.

Hand on her hip, Lou whirled on Allen. "We know your recordings picked up a conversation between Vicki and Todd about the scam they were running in the town."

Her words hit the newspaper editor like they were pieces of glass from a shattered window. He flinched, opening and closing his mouth so many times, saying nothing, that Lou ran out of patience.

"We need you to help us out, Allen. We need to hear that recording, please." Lou knew she was being forceful, so she added the softer plea at the end to appeal to the more sensitive side of him she hoped was still there.

"It could help catch Vicki and Todd's murderer." Noah stepped forward, with just as much earnestness in his tone as had been in Lou's.

Allen sighed, finally saying, "I did catch them talking, and Vicki overheard the recording one of the times she apparently hid out in my basement during her time in town. She told me she would out me as the *BSB* if I wrote anything about it." He winced. "So I stayed quiet while dozens of locals poured their hard-earned money into the pyramid scheme. I'm not proud of that, but the recording isn't going to help you figure out who killed them."

Lou swallowed. The hope she'd felt rising at his confession dropped to the floor. "Why? How do you know?" Disbelief pushed the questions forward.

Allen walked over to the small office where his computer sat. The screen was already on, and a playlist of recordings was open on the screen. "Hear for yourself." He hit play on a file, the one that had already been queued up.

"Hey," a woman's voice came through the speaker first. Vicki. Ducks quacked in the track's background, telling them this had been recorded at the park, close to the duckling enclosure. "How's everything going?"

"I saw him again." This time Todd's voice spilled out of the speaker.

Vicki groaned. "Not this again. Todd, it's fine. He's not going to do anything to us. We didn't even take it all."

"I think you're underestimating how much he cares about this." Todd's voice dropped low into a warning as he added, "You need to be faster here than usual so we can move on."

"Fine," Vicki said. "I've already got investors, and they're bringing in new people by the day."

"And you're keeping the money at the local bank?" Todd asked. "Are you sure that's smart?"

"It's fine. It helps them trust me, believe that I'm going to stick around, not bolt with their money. I'll take it out bit by bit *for expenses* or to *pay vendors* and stash it. I've got a hiding place by the bank. Then we've got it when we need to run."

Todd sighed. "Okay. I don't want to be seen with you.

Just be careful, Vick. Get as much out of these people as you can and text me when you're ready to move on."

The recording went silent for a few moments before stopping.

"That's it?" Lou asked, disappointment weighing heavily in the silence that followed.

CHAPTER 23

L ou chewed on her lip in frustration. Allen had been right. There wasn't anything concrete in the recording about the person who was following them, other than the part about how Todd was sure Vicki had underestimated how much this meant to him.

A knock sounded at the front door, and Allen's eyes flashed to Lou and Noah.

"That's Detective Anderson," Noah admitted with a grimace. "Sorry, but we thought we might need backup."

Allen's shoulders hunched. "That's okay. I should've known better than to lie to the police." He walked off to answer the door.

Lou stared at the computer screen in disbelief. She'd felt so close to figuring this out. Vicki and Todd had been caught on a recording talking about their pyramid scheme, but they hadn't said enough about whoever was following them to be of help. It *had* to be a past investor, or possibly they'd had a third partner once, and that person was mad that they'd cut them out.

Roy's deep voice spilled in from the front hallway. As they waited for Allen to bring the detective back, Lou's brain latched on to details in the room. She hadn't noticed it at first, but back here by the office, there was a lovely jasmine scent that reminded Lou of the plants outside the bookshop. Glancing around the room, Lou couldn't see any jasmine flowers in the space. She thought she remembered there being window boxes full of plants on the exterior of the house, though.

"Here they are," Allen said as he swept a hand toward Lou and Noah.

Roy's jaw was set in a tight clench. "Thanks for waiting, you two," he said sarcastically, obviously upset that they'd gone in without him.

"Sorry." Lou cringed. "It's a dead end, other than the fact that Allen here lied about knowing what Vicki and Todd were pulling on the town." She narrowed her eyes at the newspaper editor. "Do you have jasmine in your flower boxes or something?" she asked. "I just got a big whiff of it."

"Uh. No. I think those are gardenias. The jasmine smell must be from the serum. I just used some." Allen pointed to the small sample jar on the desk, just like the one almost everyone in Button had received upon Vicki's arrival.

"Oh, right." She'd gone through her own sample of the serum quickly but remembered the scent well.

"I know you said it's a dead end, but I still want to hear this file you've got saved." Roy walked over to where Lou and Noah had listened moments before. They stepped back a few feet to give Roy and Allen room in the small office.

But before she moved away, Lou plucked the bottle of Snail Serum X off the desk and glanced at the label. The sparse ingredients list mentioned a lot of proprietary mixes, but a few single ingredients jumped out at her: snail mucin, jasmine essential oil, and propolis.

Lou blinked. Propolis. Wasn't that produced by bees? She paced in the living room, gripping the bottle tight as she thought.

Then something caught her eye out the front window. Parked just past Allen's house on the street was a bright green Subaru.

Silas and Todd had both mentioned seeing a person in a beekeeper's suit driving, but Sebastian had told her tonight that Wesley saw the beekeeper in a green car.

Lou raced over to the window, peering out at the stickers covering the back bumper. One boasted that the driver had graduated from Washington State University in Pullman. Another said, "Botanists Smell Better." And a final sticker warned other drivers to "Save the Bees."

What if Allen wasn't just the editor of the local paper, but a botany enthusiast and amateur beekeeper? What if he was Vicki and Todd's third partner?

Pulling out her phone, Lou texted Noah.

> I think the killer might not be an investor.
> What if it's the creator of the serum? I think
> that person might be Allen. He's a botanist.
> His office smells like jasmine. He's into
> bees, like it says on his car out front.

Noah checked his phone. He typed back quickly.

> Let's get Roy outside and talk to him about
> the possibility.

Lou gave him a thumbs-up. They tucked their phones away and tried to look normal and nonchalant as Roy and Allen rejoined them after listening to the recording.

"Thank you, Lou and Noah, for bringing this to my attention." Roy said, this time with less sarcasm. "Allen, let me talk to the captain about this. I suppose since you've come clean now, it's better than nothing, but he might press charges since you not only committed perjury but also obstructed an active murder investigation. Two, actually."

Allen held up his hands. "I totally understand, and I will take whatever consequences come in my direction. Are you sure you don't want me to come down to the station right now?"

Roy ran a hand over his face. "Everyone needs to get some sleep. We'll figure this out in the morning."

The three of them exited Allen's home, but Lou couldn't help but notice that the newspaper editor's fingers were still shaking as he closed the door behind them.

"Roy," Lou whispered as they reached the bottom of Allen's front steps. "I think Allen might still be the killer."

Turning to face her, Roy was all hard lines in the dark. "What makes you think that?" There was a hint of frustration in his tone, but she knew he had to give her props for figuring out that Allen lied.

"What if the killer isn't an investor, but a third member of the scam? The creator of the serum." She held up the bottle she'd stolen from Allen's desk. "This contains propolis, which I know has to do with bees. Todd and Silas mentioned someone following Vicki in a beekeeping suit." She widened her eyes. "And this also contains jasmine. Not only did it smell of jasmine in there, but Allen would know a lot about using plant properties since he studied botany at Washington State."

Roy frowned. "You mean the University of Washington."

Lou's chin jutted back in surprise. "What?"

"He and I went to the same university," Roy said. "I figured it out last year when he covered the Apple Cup in the newspaper and his coverage was pro Huskies."

The big game between the two rival college football teams was a huge deal each year. Lou remembered the hubbub in town leading up to it last year.

"Huskies?" Lou asked, mentioning the University of Washington's mascot. "Then why does he have a Washington State sticker on his car?" She pointed to the red cougar sticker on the back of the green Subaru parked on the street.

Roy shook his head. "That's not Allen's car."

Lou sucked in a breath. Suddenly, she knew. The computer had already been turned on, the audio files already pulled up. Lou and Noah weren't the first ones to show up that evening, demanding to hear what information the recording contained.

"Allen's in trouble." Lou raced back up the steps. Roy and Noah followed.

This time, Lou let Roy go inside first, glad that he pulled out his gun. After quietly checking the door and finding it unlocked, they burst inside once more. The smell of jasmine now permeated the room.

Allen stood with his hands up and sweat beading on his forehead. His face was scrunched in pain like he might break into tears at any moment or possibly lose his lunch. Standing next to him was a man Lou had seen before. He held a gun to Allen's head.

"Drop the gun!" Roy said, moving in front of Lou and Noah.

But the man didn't move. Instead, he narrowed his eyes at Lou.

"You?" she asked.

"You know him?" Roy asked, keeping his eyes—and his gun—focused on the killer.

It was the man who'd come by the bookshop last week and bought a botany book.

"It wasn't the jasmine flowers I smelled that day, was it?" Lou asked.

The man snorted. "A side effect of distilling the flowers in my small lab to get the essential oils. I smell like it all the time."

Lou gasped. "You didn't come in because you wanted to adopt a cat, you heard our conversation through the screen door."

He nodded and shoved the gun deeper into Allen's temple, eyeing Roy. "Let me go and he lives. That's all I ask."

"What happened?" Lou asked in a slightly shaky voice. "You realized splitting the money three ways wasn't good enough for you? You wanted it all, so you got rid of the other two? You stalked them wearing a beekeeper's suit so no one would see your face?"

The man gritted his teeth. "I was *never* working with those two crooks. Never." He bit out the word like an insult, like a swear word. "They stole my product, the serum I'd worked the better part of a decade to perfect. Stole it right out from under me and thought they could use it in their sad little pyramid scheme." He growled, "Well, I found them. I saw Vicki sneaking around town and I followed her back to her car. Todd made it too easy by running that day. He didn't even see me coming."

His confession caught Lou by surprise. Vicki and Todd had stolen the "product" without any way to create more, but it didn't really matter since they didn't need to manufacture anything. Vicki just needed enough to put out samples to convince people it was legitimate and get them to invest.

"I can't let you go," Roy said steadily. "But it's always going to be better if you turn yourself in."

The man barked out a laugh as if Roy had just said the funniest, craziest thing he'd ever heard. His eyes were wild.

In her frantic thoughts, Lou latched on to the only thing she could think of: the silly, but effective way Todd had tricked her. She doubted this killer would fall for the bottom-of-the-shoe line, but she could try to replicate the same surprising distraction to buy them a moment or two.

Gasping, Lou screamed and pointed at the window behind Allen and the killer. "What is that?" she yelled, forcing her face into a surprised grimace.

It worked. Not only did the killer turn to look over his shoulder, but Allen jumped in surprise. The movement knocked the gun out of the killer's hands, and it clattered to the floor. Roy shot across the room and was on the man in an instant. He had his knee in his back and his handcuffs out within seconds.

Lou breathed a sigh of immense relief. She closed her eyes as Noah pulled her into a tight hug.

CHAPTER 24

Lou knew she didn't need to open the bookshop the following day, but after the night they'd had, she needed a little normalcy.

The news was all over the town, mostly because the *BSB* had written one final post. It had been an unmasking, a confession, an apology, and one last piece of local gossip all rolled into one.

My Last Post

Dear people of Button, this will be my final post on Behind the Scenes in Button. *I started this blog at a low place. I was frustrated to see the continually dropping sales numbers at the* Button Post *and knew our online subscriptions weren't enough to keep the paper going. With a town so focused on gossip, I wondered how an anonymous blog about more trivial matters might perform. At first, I tried out starting baseless rumors, but I soon found that readers would send me gossip in anonymous emails through the contact form on my site, and I didn't need to make anything up.*

I was blown away by the popularity of the BSB blog.

As it continued, I realized two things: 1. I might use a segment such as this to save the newspaper and 2. I was going to need better access to the town's secrets (as I was running low on them as the weeks went on).

And here is where my first apology comes in. I'm sorry that I listened in on conversations that were not mine to hear. Because I've spent the last handful of weeks entrenched in it, I know the local gossip mill will have done its job by now and you know that I placed recording devices around town. I'm so sorry for that invasion of privacy.

Which brings me to my second apology. One such conversation I overheard was, in fact, the late Vicki and her partner in crime, discussing the scam they were pulling on the people of our town. I said nothing because she got to me first and threatened to release my identity. I'm so sorry.

And that brings me to my last point. I, Allen Kettle, will step down as the editor-in-chief of the Button Post, *effective immediately. Once you have a botanist-turned-killer hide in your closet while the police inspect your computer files, you reevaluate decisions you've made. As for now, I'm glad the good people of this town are most likely going to get their money returned to them. I will stay around unless it becomes clear I'm not welcome. Wouldn't want to make that mistake again.*

Thank you to Louisa Henry and Noah Ramero for the double-back of the century. I'm grateful I wasn't alone with Peter Greer for long. Farewell for now.

Lou had to smile at Allen's mention of staying in town even though he wasn't welcome, like Ronald Rossback, the man who used to live in the decrepit mansion on Thread

Lane. She also knew the sparse amount of information he'd included about the killer, Peter Greer, would only serve to generate questions among the locals.

Because of that, and the fact that both Lou and Noah were mentioned in the post, Lou expected the bookshop would be hopping, and she wasn't above using town drama to drum up book sales.

As Lou headed downstairs that morning, she found someone waiting at the front door of the bookshop. But it wasn't Silas whom she'd expected, now that he was officially cleared and free to come back. It was Detective Roy Anderson.

Lou hurried over and unlocked the door, letting Roy inside. "Hey, is everything okay with the case?"

"Everything's fine." Roy looked like he'd gotten all of five minutes of shut-eye since she last saw him. "Peter confessed to everything in front of the captain and me last night. Cap's not too happy about Allen's last post as the *BSB*, but he'll get over it." He glanced down. "I actually wanted to come by and let you know that I'm leaving town."

Lou sucked in a surprised breath. "Not because of this case, right?" She always liked to think that she was helping with investigations. It was never her intention to hurt the people tasked with solving them.

Roy shook his head vehemently to stop her worries. "Carly got a job in Olympia, and I'm going to move with her."

Carly Zimmerman, Roy's girlfriend, had lost her position at the local high school at the end of that school year, partly because she'd made some costly mistakes and partly because the horticulture position just didn't have the funding to continue. She'd been on the search for a new job all summer.

"There's a station down there that'll take me. The captain wasn't sure she'd have room, at first, but after hearing about my arrest of Peter last night, she said she'd figure it out." Roy's chest puffed out a little with pride. "So … thank you for helping. I can honestly say I wouldn't have caught him without you."

It was all so kind, especially coming from Roy. "You're welcome. We're going to miss you around here, though." Lou mentally snapped her fingers. Of course he had to leave. Just when the man was trusting her and feeling like one of the locals.

"Willow and I grew up around Olympia, and her parents still live down there, so let us know if you want any recommendations." Lou grinned. "When do you leave?"

He puffed out his cheeks. "Carly's already packed and headed down to search for a rental. I'm going to stick around until this case finishes up. I just wanted you to hear it from me, not the local gossip mill." He winked at her.

Lou laughed. "I appreciate that. Once Easton and Willow get back, we'll have to do a dinner again with the six of us."

They'd tried before, but Roy had been dating someone else at the time, and things hadn't ended well. Lou had much higher hopes for a second try. She and Noah would still have to go as friends, of course, but just the thought of spending time with him still made her whole body hum with happiness.

"Sounds good." Roy gave her a salute and turned to leave.

Just as Roy was leaving, Silas ambled up to the bookshop, a newspaper tucked under his arm. He grunted a greeting to Roy, shooting him a bit of a glare to remind him he hadn't forgotten his time in the police station.

"Morning, Silas." Lou waved goodbye to Roy and turned it into a greeting for Silas. "Glad to have you back."

George came crashing in after Silas. It was a good thing the young woman wasn't wearing her cat that day because he would've been crushed in the tight hug George gave Lou as she told her she was glad she was okay and that she needed to hear the entire story about what had happened in Allen Kettle's house last night. Cricket and Forrest repeated the sentiment when they bustled in after George. Lou resigned herself to the fact that she would have to retell the story many times that day.

When a black sedan pulled up, Lou knew word had reached Sebastian up on the hill. She wasn't surprised when Wesley followed the millionaire out of the car, his thumbs hooked on to the belt loops of garishly bright-pink shorts with little red lobsters on them.

"What are you doing here?" George shoved an accusatory finger toward Wesley.

"You know Sebastian's PI?" Lou asked.

Wesley and George scoffed in unison.

"He was my terrible date from the other night," she said.

Cricket let out a low whistle. "This just got good."

"The one you left before the appetizers came because it was such a bust?" Silas asked.

Wesley held up a finger. "A mutual bust, by the way. We both felt that there was no connection." He moved his finger back and forth between them.

George narrowed her eyes at him, but Sebastian interrupted.

"I heard about the arrest through Wesley, but that's not the reason I'm here." Sebastian cleared his throat. "I also heard the quilting convention lost its sponsors."

Cricket, the only quilting representative present, stood, but her mouth just hung open.

Sebastian faced her anyway. "I would like to officially step in as the event's sole sponsor. Someone wise recently told me that the best way to get myself out there is to get involved, invest myself in the town." He glanced at Lou. "Oh, I also bought the *Button Post* this morning," he added.

"I told you the town doesn't only care about your money, Sebastian. You don't have to buy up everything in need," Lou said, blinking in surprise.

"But it's what I do best. Plus, I want to." Sebastian beamed. "You gave me a sense of what it was like to be involved in my community, and I guess I just couldn't get enough."

Lou started clapping and everyone joined in. The cats didn't appreciate the noise, though, and they scattered—except for Sapphire, the only one who couldn't hear the commotion.

Willow and Easton strode through the door as the clapping reached a crescendo. "Awww. For us?" Willow joked, placing a hand on her collarbone.

Lou raced over to envelop her friend in a hug. "It's a long story," she said after she pulled back.

Once introductions were made between those who'd yet to meet, everyone filled Willow and Easton in on what they'd missed the night before. Lou let George tell most of the story since she seemed willing. The few times George got details wrong, Lou didn't even have time to correct her because Wesley jumped in with the amendments. Each time he did, George shot him a look that Lou was sure could've done physical harm.

"I think we all believe you two about the lack in chemistry," Cricket said after Wesley's last interruption led into a heated argument between the two twentysomethings.

"Wait. These two dated?" Willow asked Lou. When she nodded, Willow mumbled, "Apparently, I've missed *a lot*."

Lou widened her eyes. "You have no idea. Want to take a walk? I can close up for an hour or so."

George stepped forward. "Don't worry. I'll watch the place. You two go catch up."

Lou thanked George profusely before dragging Willow outside. Hooking her arm through Willow's, they walked down Thread Lane. Lou waited until they were far enough away from the bookshop's screen door to start talking, not about to make that mistake again. Once they were, she told her about Noah showing up last night and what they'd talked about in terms of keeping things quiet for a while.

Her best friend's squeal of happiness could be heard throughout the quiet town.

WHISKERS AND WORDS WILL RETURN ...

He went too *fur*.

The town of Button, Washington is already as "cute as a button" with its sewing themed streets, quaint buildings, and colorful pastel window trimmings. But Godfrey Crane thinks the town can be even better. That's why he founds the Button Beatification Society. From its inception, the organization receives vocal opposition from locals, especially one of Louisa's bookshop regulars, Cricket.

Cricket doesn't hold back when it comes to Godfrey and his organization, so when Lou finds the man murdered, all eyes turn to Cricket. Even though she has an alibi, she's not out of trouble yet. Convinced that the killer came from within his own organization, Cricket hatches a plan to infiltrate the Beautification Society and use the murder to take it down once and for all. She enlists Lou and her friends to help. And while Lou tags along mostly to keep Cricket safe, she quickly feels like she's in too deep and worries if any of them will get out alive.

Coming fall 2023
Get your copy

Join Eryn Scott's mailing list to learn about new releases and sales!

Whiskers and Words Mysteries

Ongoing series * Best friends *
Bookshop full of cats

PEPPER BROOKS
COZY MYSTERY SERIES

Completed series * Literary mysteries * Sweet romance * Cute dog

ABOUT THE AUTHOR

Eryn Scott lives in the Pacific Northwest with her husband and their quirky animals. She loves classic literature, musicals, knitting, and hiking. She writes cozy mysteries and women's fiction.

Join her mailing list to learn about new releases and sales!

www.erynscott.com